The Harvester

A Trap Jones

BLOOD BOUND BOOKS

Copyright © 2015 by K. Trap Jones
All rights reserved

ISBN 978-1-940250-18-2

Artwork by Andrej Bartulovic

Interior Layout by Lori Michelle

Printed in the United States of America

First Edition

Visit us on the web at:
www.bloodboundbooks.net

Also from Blood Bound Books:

400 Days of Oppression by Wrath James White
Habeas Corpse by Nikki Hopeman
Loveless by Dev Jarrett
The Sinner by K. Trap Jones
Mother's Boys by Daniel I. Russell
Knuckle Supper by Drew Stepek
Sons of the Pope by Daniel O'Connor
Dolls by KJ Moore
At the End of All Things by Stony Graves
The Return by David A Riley
Fallow Ground by Michael James McFarland
The Black Land by MJ Wesolowski
Cradle of the Dead by Roger Jackson
Dark Waves by Simon Kearns

For my wife Robyn and my three sons: Chase, Hunter and Ayden.

When a man lies. He murders some
    part of the world.
These are the pale deaths which men
    miscall their lives.
All this I cannot bear to witness
    any longer.
Cannot the Kingdom of Salvation
    take me home?

—Paul Gerhardt (1607–1667)
—Adapted by Cliff Burton (1962–1986)
To Live Is To Die, Metallica (1988)

Preface

Released from his isolation, the farmer chosen by God to test the boundaries of the seven deadly sins and their associated demons is burdened with the task of unleashing sin upon mankind. The following are his seven translated entries within their original narrative state.

I: Depression

As I wait and bleed,
Hidden well within my darkened cave,
The angels of Heaven converge down upon me.
Servants of God, burdened with the task of my retrieval.
I have displeased God and his hand of vengeance
Seeks to punish me for the path I have chosen to travel.

All of my fellow demons are gone,
Stolen by angels through the cracks in the sky.
My realm lays in ruins,
Littered with the corpses of my enemies.
My palace has been reaped from the cavern.
All hope is gone, all for the choices I have made.
I have sought shelter within the trenches of my kingdom
So that I may continue my tale.

Many centuries have passed
Since I last held this quill within my hand.
It greets me like a long lost friend
And shows eagerness to begin a new relationship.
One not forged from fear,
But united in conviction and companionship.
My earlier entries spoke of confusion and resentment.
You will find none of that now.

The Harvester

If it is the truth that you seek,
    Then you shall discover it.
    If it is understanding that you desire,
    It will greet you unconditionally.

One must first comprehend the path in which I chose.
    One must first dive down within the pit of my kingdom,
    Into the belly of the beast where you will know my rise.
    Let us begin first where I ended; my release from the cave.
    I must hurry, as I can hear the angels approaching.

Remembering my name of Satan
    Was a blessing, but like all blessings,
    It was short lived.
    After successfully testing the boundaries
    Of the seven deadly sins, I was allowed freedom.

The confusion about my new task
    Of releasing sin upon mankind
    Weighed heavy upon my mind, so much so
    That I entered a state of sheer depression.
    Roaming aimlessly without direction,
    I came upon a small village in search of wine.

The mere thought of the sweet nectar
    Moistened my mouth and salivated my visions.
    To have it pass through my lips
    And coat my tongue inspired me.

I noticed a lone villager stumbling, his speech slurred.
    With his hands outreached, he spoke in broken words.
    I was not interested in his language
    But his mouth leaked the aroma I desired.

Jones

Through his rambling,
    I asked him to show me where he had been.
    His obliged and led me from the courtyard
    Toward the handle of a door within a small inlet.
    The smell of the scent invigorated my senses,
    Like a warm breeze winding through a field of fruit.

My friend pushed through the thickened wooden door
    As a gust of sweet nectar caressed my face.
    Upon my entrance, I was greeted by stares.
    Their eyes meant nothing, but still they judged,
    Deciphering my very being to see if I was like them.
    I looked none of them in the eye,
    As they were obstacles on my quest for liquid goodness.
    I sat alongside my friend as a large burly man
    Placed a goblet sloshing with red wine in front of me.
    Through my nose the smell traveled;
    My eyes closing with each inhale.

With each swig, I felt my mind wander.
    I was set adrift in a vast sea of disillusion.
    I drank more in hopes to relieve my mind.
    However, the next four brought about a depression
    Of which I would never recover.
    The edge between turmoil and realism became distant.
    The canyon widened with every drop that slid down my throat.
    My heart became full of sorrow and remorse
    For memories I could not claim as my own.
    Visions of a city;
    Depictions of large caverns and a troubled river
    Plagued the decayed walls of where I resided.
    I could not understand them nor relate, but they felt true.
    The far wall crumbled, revealing
    A large field spanning as far as I could see.
    The land was littered with bones,
    Trampled upon by crowds of souls

The Harvester

Roaming aimlessly in the same direction.
I turned back around to shelter myself.
I felt that what I was seeing were not *my* memories,
But those of someone else.

I shifted and looked again.
 A labyrinth pf darkness replaced the fields.
 The blackness disrupted my stomach as I held my chest.

The pain of my existence became unbearable.
 My mind offered me no friendly advice;
 Instead, it merely tormented me with more visions.
 The pain and suffering I endured
 Ventured back to me as I tipped the goblet.

Every gulp, every drop of the poison
 Clouded my reasoning and butchered my dreams.
 I drank to forget, but it would also serve
 As the source of my remembrance.

I saw the serpent of anger swimming around in circles
 Within the red sea of the goblet
 But still I drank from the contaminated source.
 I felt the serpent wind its way down my throat.
 I was seeking blindness; instead I received full vision.

More serpents slithered through the door
 With elongated bodies that entwined themselves
 Amongst the legs of the people and chairs.
 Their mouths hissing as they moved.
 Their forked tongues lashing out to touch the ankles.

The shadows shifted in the room
 Without the change of sun.
 The candles flickered
 Without the help from the wind.

Jones

The mouths of the villagers were moving,
But no sound was heard.
I turned to my newfound friend
As his lips rambled at a fast pace.
I stared at his tongue in hopes to hear,
But my ears were deceiving me.
A crackling noise, so distinct, grabbed my attention.
I looked closely to my goblet
As I saw small cracks etch along the metal.
Red droplets leaked through and fell down the stem.

Strange happenings were stirring,
    Some of my past, some I could not understand.
    My studies of the seven sins seeped into the place
    And sidled up to me like an unwelcome guest.

The bitter remorse and heavy damnation
    Of my thoughts shielded my judgment
    And twisted my visions away from an understanding.
    I began to question myself
    And resented my mind for what it was portraying.
    The villagers each transformed into a figure of my past.
    Amon and Beelzebub sat against the near wall.
    Leviathan and Asmodeus spoke in the corner.
    Mammon and Belphegor had just walked in.
    And Lucifer served me from behind the counter.

Not only the demons, but more appeared.
    The wealthy man I killed in wrath, stood by me
    With my daggers still protruding from his chest.
    The beloved maiden of lust appeared
    Holding her heart within her hands,
    Pleading with me to make her whole again.

The Harvester

I could not decipher whether the visions were real,
    So I accepted another goblet of wine from Lucifer
    And tried to make a truce with my troubled mind.

I closed my eyes to pray for the gift of reasoning.
    God answered me with more rapid visions
    Of death and betrayal; all by my hands.
    I held my head in hopes to ease the pain.
    I could sense them surrounding me.
    I kept my eyes sealed shut.
    I wanted to kill them all.
    I wanted to watch them all die a slow death;
    To clench each of their throats
    Until their eyes rolled back into their heads.

My skin boiled from their nearness.
    Suffocation by sharing the same air
    Trembled my hands and had me seeking a way out.

Instead, I simply opened my eyes.
    Surrounded by people,
    My arm was engulfed in flames.

Their eyes were upon me with an astonished gaze.
    Questions, as to why I felt no pain,
    Spilled from the crowd.

I hesitantly looked down to my arm
    With my clothing frayed and my flesh melting.
    It was true, I felt no pain.

I saw one demon from my past staring back at me.
    Lucifer smiled while holding a candle.
    No reasoning was said, no reaction was given.
    He simply vanished and left me alone to explain.

Jones

The other villagers did not leave as quickly.
    They tried to rationally think of a reason
    As to why I had no reaction to a burning arm.
    My friend, however, offered a solution
    That would not serve me well.
    He mentioned a tale of a demon so vile
    That fire could not scar him.
    Silence fell upon the room
    As my own judging eyes pierced his skull.
    The others settled on the same assumption.
    Apparently, they did not care for demons;
    I was immediately grabbed by the angry mob
    And dragged to the floor
    Where they secured each of my limbs.

I made it easy for them.
    My depression was in full control of my mind;
    Therefore I offered no fight.
    Maybe they could provide me with what I wanted:
    A simple death.

My troubled emotions allowed the attacks,
    But they would have to use more
    To even stir my conscience.
    I had been through much worse;
    I would not be threatened by mortal hands.

With their fists and feet becoming bruised,
    And their mouths gasping for air,
    They used chairs and table legs to inflict more pain.

When the physical onslaught proved unsuccessful,
    They pulled my body outside
    Toward the river that flowed next to the village.
    Two large men dragged me into the water.

The Harvester

Without remorse, they submerged me with ease.
    Again, I offered no fight.
    Maybe my immortality could be removed by the water.
    I figured I would allow them to try.
    My body became limp, not due to death,
    But rather because of my lack of care.
    A gasp came over the crowd watching ashore
    When I was lifted from the water and smiled at them.

My two captors submerged me again.
    It was quiet and peaceful under the surface
    As the water sealed my ears.
    The annoying chatter was replaced
    With the sublime sound of silence.
    The coolness of the water soothed my skin
    And offered tranquility to my healing bones.
    With no sounds to be heard, the beating of my slowing heart
    Provided a rhythm and something tangible to relate to.
    Instead of holding my breath, I opened my mouth
    To allow the water to freely flow down my throat.
    Drowning was not my first choice for death,
    But under the circumstances,
    I thought I had nothing else to lose.

They interrupted my serenity by lifting me up again.
    One of them turned my face hoping to see me dead,
    But a raised eyebrow was what I provided.

At that point, all doubts of my demon ability had vanished.
    Even the non-believers were reassured.
    The river was not the answer,
    So I was dragged back up the rocky river bank.
    My skin tore across the jagged terrain.

Back into the courtyard we went
    Where I was held by my throat against a column

Jones

While my arms were pulled backwards and bound.
Satisfied with my imprisonment and inability to move,
They talked about what fate I should have next.

Branches and rotted brush were piled at my feet
    With a ring of torch bearing men standing near.
    Their idea was to burn my demon corpse
    And send the remnants of my soul to God.
    God would be ever thankful
    To each who took the life of a demon.
    The ideas were the basis for my slaughter;
    The reasoning behind the madness of the situation.

As the torches lit up their faces,
    I gazed upon their mannerisms
    For a sense of remorse or pity.
    Much like in the river, I found none.
    As I watched the torches fall upon the kindling,
    I was enamored by the twirling smoke trails.
    The fire rose to collect my lower clothing as its own
    With the smoke blackening from the material.
    The observers were getting impatient.
    My reaction was not what they had envisioned.
    My death would not come through fire.
    The heat singed my flesh, but offered me no harm.

Still believing in an obscured concept,
    They smoldered the blaze with water.
    Through the damp, thickened smoke, I could see that
    A new plan was being accepted.

Again they gathered directly in front of the column
    For a brief meeting about my demise.
    I saw one of them run off into a nearby house.
    He soon reappeared with a wooden stake.

The Harvester

They passed the stake between them
    As no one had the courage for the task at hand.
    It fell to the ground with no one claiming ownership.
    Frustration attacked the crowd as they feared
    The disappointment of God
    And the suffering they would all endure as a result.

A large brawny man appeared and grabbed the stake.
    With words of appeasing God,
    He held the stake up high for all to see.
    Silence fell within the courtyard
    With no one fighting the decision
    As there were no other volunteers.

He stepped before me with a little hesitation.
    He reminded me of myself
    With eyes of coal and a heavy hand.
    A moment of calm came over the crowd
    Wondering whether the man was up for the task.
    My appearance proved difficult for him;
    I was not the sharpened tooth, ravenous beast
    That their minds imagined me as.

My flesh was that of theirs;
    My bone was that of theirs;
    My speech was that of theirs,
    But my mind and soul were not.

The man demanded my face be hidden.
    He did not want to see my eyes while murdering me.
    An act of kindness on my part or weakness on his.
    Either had no real meaning to me.

The chosen one walked out of sight, before returning
    With a brown satchel saturated with blood,
    So much so that excess left a trail.

Jones

The man walked up to me with a disgusted look
    Embedded on his face as he reached inside,
    Revealing a severed goat's head.

The weak stomachs of the crowd showed no mercy.
    My initial thought was why the village would have had
    A severed goat's head available?

The hero raised the remains and slowly
    Slid the flesh and skull of the animal over mine.
    Granted, I had experienced a lot of insanity in my time,
    But the dead, cool flesh suctioning to my face
    Would remain with me for quite some time.
    Once I became used to the smell, I opened my eyes
    Allowing me sight through the sockets of the goat.
    My breath forged a path through the mouth crevice.
    I had no choice, but to taste the carcass on my lips.
    The blood of the animal found its way
    Within my nostrils and around my tongue.
    The surplus amounts were spit through the mouth hole
    As the taste was not to my liking.

Feeling the pressure from the eyes of his peers,
    The man tore my frayed shirt to expose my bare chest.
    He held the sharpened weapon,
    Searching for my beating heart.
    My breath through the goat's mouth
    Prompted his backward sway from me.
    As I was finding sanctuary within the hallowed head,
    Others did not share the same unification ritual as I.

With more disgust than anguish,
    He leaned back and plunged
    The wooden stake deep into my heart.
    I saw the eyes of the man
    As my blood splashed against his face.

The Harvester

With his energy flowing,
    He twisted the wood deep within me.
    I felt the pain; I felt the distress of the crowd,
    But I did not feel the arrival of death.

The man stepped back as my blood pooled beneath me.
    The mob was satisfied and cheered the man.
    If I bled, I would die.
    Even seemed rational to me,
    But my blood was not like theirs.
    I was not like any of them.

They left me there to rot in the night air
    As they slept peacefully in their abodes.
    Tied to the column as a goat; a trophy of a capture.
    The crows flew to me tempted either by my blood
    Or the aroma gifted to the air by the severed head.
    Regardless of their reasoning, they arrived.
    I could feel them all around, landing upon me.
    Their claws gripping my flesh for support.
    My mask was being tugged as they pecked for food.
    My neck constantly shifted
    Becoming a victim to the movement of the goat skull.

Night wolves also roamed near.
    The crows took to higher ground.
    Two grey wolves approached with caution,
    Their curious noses filled with the scent of my wounds.
    The puddles of my own blood kept them at a distance
    And appeased their carnivorous appetites.
    As strange as it may sound,
    I did find some comfort in watching them drink.

Their lips curled, allowing their teeth to grip the flesh.
    When the greediness of the wolves turned to hunger,
    My eyes met with the yellow pupils of my enemies.

Jones

Their ears bent back, their snout wrinkled.
With slow precise leg movement; they wanted to feast.
Their heavy paws crept ever so slowly
In my direction with a low growl of anticipation.

My salvation came in the form
Of a lone lightning bolt extending down from the sky.
The collision with the courtyard
Sent sparks that attacked both wolves.
The wolves whelped as they scampered off into the trees.
My destiny was not to be devoured by nature.

The next sun, I became a relic;
A village spectacle, as each viewed me as a slain demon.
God's work had been achieved with gifts of glory
To be descended upon them.

I looked upon their smiles and satisfaction with disgust.
Their laughter echoed through my bones;
Their rude gestures clinched my muscles,
But my depression took precedent.
It carved my insides with its long reach
And twisted my thoughts with visions of sorrow.

My body could not counter the emotion.
All physical movements were rendered with weakness
Compared to the onslaught on my emotional mind.
I often rotated my arms,
Not to gain release from my bindings,
But to reach a more comfortable position.

The dry, rough rope tore at my wrists,
But I felt no pain.
The wooden stake lay deep within my chest,
But I felt no pain.
My mind was my true enemy now.

The Harvester

With my body secured, my mind became relentless.
I reached the edge of insanity
As I resided against the column,
Barely able to breathe through my mask.

My body, in an attempt for freedom, shook uncontrollably.
    The violent nature of the movement scared some away.

As my blood continued to drip,
    So did the passing of the sun.
    Through the hallowed out sockets of the goat's eyes,
    I watched it hide behind the mountains.
    I remember feeling peace;
    A calmness for the approaching night.
    Hoping that the darkness would heal my body.
    Hope was not always attainable,
    But when it did reveal itself,
    I welcomed it wholeheartedly.
    To believe that all hope was gone
    Would be dissatisfaction with God.

I chewed at the goat's mouth
    In order to widen the hole in which I breathed.
    Spitting the excess out,
    I was able to increase my access to the night air.
    The deep breaths were beautiful
    And my lungs were quite thankful.

Even though I was still imprisoned within a village
    By people bent on watching me die,
    I held tightly to my small piece
    Of tranquility with every breath I took.

As the stars appeared, most of the crowd dispersed,
    But a few stayed to throw rocks and tainted food at me.
    I found myself struggling to receive a restful state.

Jones

I could no longer move my legs,
But could feel the breeze flowing over my wounds.
I focused on the sensation
And was able to find a peaceful slumber of sorts.

My body had seen much worse.
    The presence of pain was everlasting.
    Although I had become accustomed,
    I often desired for my body to be left alone.
    Sleep provided me with an escape from persecution.
    My heart still thrived despite the wooden stake.
    The once flowing stream of my blood slowed.
    The loss was every drop I could offer.
    I felt close to death.
    I looked down into my own grave,
    As if I was a part of a mortal death.
    My corpse, hands crossed upon my chest, eyes closed;
    I was content.
    No wounds, no scars, no torment, only contentment.
    No demons were with him.
    No sins were with him.
    My corpse was alone with his thoughts.

Not knowing how long I slept,
    I was awoken by a prodding to my leg.
    The goat's blood had sealed my eyelids shut,
    But with a little effort, I was able to open them.

A small child was determined to awaken me with a branch.
    If my legs were not tied, I would have kicked him away.
    When he noticed my attention,
    He raised his branch and gestured.
    Through the decayed flesh,
    I saw a distant person walking towards the village.

The Harvester

The boy quickly ran from the courtyard.
    Then I heard it; that faint singing.
    I was gripped by intense fear.
    All other emotions paled in comparison.
    She was coming, my captor in the cave.
    I had never laid eyes on her before
    As she hid well within the darkness, but her song
    Made my heart bleed with every hymn.
    She would sing whenever she was near.
    Whenever I had doubt, she would come.
    Whenever I lost faith, she would come.

I immediately struggled for my freedom.
    I felt the goat's head twist from the fight.
    Stopping to judge her distance,
    Her hymn was becoming louder.

I was not alone in my vision of her.
    Several of the villagers noticed her as well.
    I had never seen her outside of the darkness.
    She was always hidden within the cave shadows.
    The closer she became, the more of her I could see.
    I envisioned my shadowy captor as a hag or witch,
    So demonic that one would not dare lay eyes upon.
    A horrific beast forged from God's anger.
    But she was none of those.
    She was strikingly beautiful to behold with an essence
    That demanded both the attention and respect
    For God's ability to create.

I was blinded by her splendor.
    With every step closer, she became more stunning.
    Her song consumed my senses
    And calmed the fear of my soul.

Jones

What I witnessed next will be difficult to transcribe
  As even now, I cannot truly comprehend it.
  I witnessed sheer terror, of which still haunts me.

Even the moon hid behind the clouds.
  No other noises existed; not from the wind or nature.
  Just her song; a melody of resentment and agony.
  The ties that bound me tightened.
  The hallowed head of the animal shifted upward
  So that my eyes were staring directly down the path.
  I gaped in awe at her flowing white gown.
  Her long hair danced so eloquently in the night.

Her voyage continued with the villagers all enamored.
  Her pale complexion glistened in the moonlight
  Like a sparkling ocean in the sun.
  Her aura made me forget my memories.

She was within the village perimeter.
  I could see her eyes fixated upon me.
  I could not turn my head to look away.
  I noticed one of the villagers walking towards her.
  Without warning and without taking her eyes off me,
  His body became distorted.
  His head bent backward, his arms twisted behind him,
  Every bone went the opposite way,
  But yet he remained standing, still alive.
  I could hear him struggle for breath.
  There were no screams, no tears.
  His mind and body did not know how to react.
  He became suspended in the air,
  Hiis mind a prisoner of his tangled flesh.
  His eyes could only roam aimlessly,
  His tongue moved uncontrollably.
  No speech, no sound, emitted from his lips.
  He was taken to the boundary of death,

The Harvester

I could see his mind trying to decipher his visions,
Desperately seeking to understand.
As she continued walking, his neck was broken.

She did not lose stride in her approach,
    Even as another village tested his fate.
    Every limb of the man was twisted.
    His head, arms and legs did a full rotation.
    His flesh ripped under the pressure.
    No scream, no exhaust of pain was heard.
    He simply slumped to a pile on the ground.
    Her beauty was a power which one could dwell within;
    Sacrifice their lives for a closer glimpse.
    I was not immune either, but seeing the demonic deaths
    Prompted me to continue to seek release.

Through my struggle, I saw another villager approach her.
    His limbs were ripped and thrown a great distance.
    His torso was the only portion that remained.

One villager was lifted into the air and his spine was ripped
    From his body through his mouth.
    Both pieces fell to the ground as she continued walking.

I pleaded to the skies to unbind me,
    But the clouds offered a thunderous laughter.
    My worry was captured in the streaks of lightning
    Splitting the sky with such ferocity and despair.

As she strolled gracefully upon the path,
    My mind hid from any rational understanding.
    It left me with only the thought of death,
    Not by the will power of the villagers,
    But from the hand of God.

Jones

My emotions were troubled and lost.
    I could not control them any longer.
    My body was at the mercy of a mindless soul.

My eyes swelled and watered
    Hoping to somehow ease my damaged mind.
    Tears streamed from beneath my mask
    As I looked once again to the skies.
    I begged for mercy; I begged for a quick death.

Instead of salvation, the skies mocked my sadness
    With a downpour of its own.
    The rain drops pelted my body
    As my head sagged away from the column.

With her close, the control over my mind departed.
    I was no longer scared; I was no longer ashamed.
    I was merely content.
    My thoughts spoke of a beautiful death,
    One that would calm my distressed thoughts.
    One that would halt the deathly visions for once.

A death so wonderful that no man would turn away from.
    An existence of pure peace with no suffering.

The revelation calmed my heart and soothed my blood.
    I said no words, but again pleaded with God.
    I heard my fate in the rhythm of her song.
    I saw my fate in the stride of her walk.
    I smelled my fate in the aroma of her skin.

If I had never felt her pain,
    I would have been charmed by her.
    Her essence was truly beautiful to behold,
    But I knew what was under her veil.
    The hatred, the chaos, the infliction.
    I had known it well; the others did not.

The Harvester

Where the villagers failed in my death,
    She would be victorious.
    I welcomed her for a first
    As I hoped she carried a gift for me.
    She stood before me
    As a goddess sent by God.

With a handful of goat hair, she slid the hallowed head off.
    The flesh gripped my face, opening my mouth.
    It left behind a coating of red on my skin.
    The moisture of the blood felt cold against the wind,
    But the air tasted sweet in comparison.
    The mask had provided me a sort of sanctuary.
    Without it, I felt vulnerable and weak.

Being face to face with her was breathtaking.
    It made me unsure as to whether she was my enemy.
    I could only stare and lose myself within her spirit.
    She raised her hand to me, not to split my skull,
    But rather to caress my face with her palm.
    Her hands were soft against my scarred wounds.
    I found myself leaning into her touch,
    Getting lost within her eyes.
    I wanted to see the visions
    That she had seen within God's kingdom.
    I wanted to stroke the cloth she wore.
    She was my angel sent from God.
    She was my guide, my liberator.

Her eyes were filled with compassion.
    Her mannerisms prompted by understanding.
    Her touch was redemption for all of the pain.
    Her care was a blessing, but short lived.

She quickly extracted the stake from my chest.
    The pain was sudden and drained my lungs of air.

Jones

Blood sprayed upon her white, flowing gown.

Her appearance never altered,
    But her eyes turned a deep hue of red.
    Her mouth produced a snarl
    That would deter an angry pack of lions.

With a quick jab of her palm,
    My head snapped backwards, splitting the column.
    My vision blurred; my skull swayed.
    I felt blood spilling from my nose.

She presented her hands before me.
    As I watched through a haze, her fingernails grew.
    With no hesitation,
    She gored both of her hands deep within me.
    She pried my chest apart,
    Pulling at both sections of my ribcage.
    My skin splintered from the power
    And gave way to my dissection.

The wind chilled my internal organs
    As her head lowered to look inside me.
    Her hand grasped my still beating heart,
    Judging my well-being with her eyes.

Satisfied with her findings, she grabbed my outer torso
    And applied pressure to close my rib cage.
    My bones twisted and snapped.
    Let it be known, that she did not
    Return my body to its previous state.

Her appearance had changed
    As if she had waded in a river of my own blood.
    The ropes that held me, loosened and fell.
    My lungs were struggling for breath,

The Harvester

Even though they were exposed to the night air.
Her other hand rested on my temple.
She was reading me; my mind, my spirit.
Seeing if my soul was still able for the task.

Without much thought or concern,
My mind spoke two words:
No more.
She heard my thought
As an evil grin stretched from ear to ear.

As she suspended me by my neck,
I knew I had made a mistake.
I demanded from her, when I should not have.

As I flew through the air,
I remember thinking about exiting that cave.
It was a grain of happiness;
Overshadowed by visions of my farm.
That image became my strength; my backbone.
That first breath of fresh air and warmth of the sun
Rejuvenated the very essence of my soul.
As my body collided with a nearby roof,
I dwelled in the moment that I realized I was immortal.
I smiled at the irony while she pounced on me,
Shattering my right leg.
Receiving the acceptance of the seven demons
Was a gift I held close,
Even when she dragged me through the mud.

I had come so far, but gone nowhere.
The smell of my old wheat fields teased my senses,
As she dropped me down on a wooden fence post.

None of it mattered to me anymore.
She could have my body;

Jones

She could have all my physical traits,
But she would never steal my memories.

I prayed to not see my torture,
    But she held me close to death at all times,
    So close that I could see angels in a valley of green.
    Before I could linger, she pulled me back to reality;
    Back to that darkened village of hatred.

As she slammed my head deep into the ground,
    I saw visions of trees ripened with lush apples
    So red that they stood apart from the green leaves.

I saw the muddy ground from my upside down state.
    My fingers sliding across, collecting dirt.

I met the outside wall of a building with vengeance,
    With my body proving to not be the victor in the battle.
    White clouds danced within the sky.
    No storms, no rain, no lightning.

The pressure she applied as she gripped my skull
    Went deeper than skin; deeper than bone.
    I could feel her nails upon my brain.
    My body followed my head
    As she slammed my face into many obstacles.
    I wished for a quick death,
    Instead I was granted eyes that would not close.

She was not allowed to kill me.
    She was not allowed to gift me what I wanted.

Ironically, I was enlightened with humor.
    My bruised organs made it difficult, but I was laughing.
    My disrespect would not be tolerated.
    No pain, no agony or anguish would ever change that.

The Harvester

I hated her for what she was.
I hated her for what she was tasked to do.
I hated her because she enjoyed it.

She lifted me and held my face close.
    Through one eye, I saw her frustration.
    I saw her anxiety with me not allowing her to succeed.

I landed in the mud of the pig sty.
    The friendly creatures allowed me room.
    Small acts of kindness in such a horrible place.
    Upon the arrival of my enemy,
    Their large bellies were split in two and tossed aside.
    By my ankle, I left the mud.

With her fingers gripped around my neck,
    She lifted my bruised body.
    Her eyes were still as beautiful as ever;
    Mine could barely be opened.

She wanted to break my will.
    Hidden within me was a severely shattered will,
    But I would not allow her to prosper from it.
    My demeanor was that of a victorious king
    Although my body did not reflect the same.

She held me close to study me once again,
    But, before she could see the truth,
    I prompted her into a new direction.
    As anger sank deep within my mind,
    I gathered any lose saliva and spit directly in her face.
    She flinched, dropped me where she stood.
    With my body in shambles, I could not move.
    I could only wait for her reaction.
    The blood mixture smeared across her perfect skin.

Jones

Could she be tempted away from God?
    Her anger was well noted, but how far could she go?
    The villagers could have never killed me,
    But she had the potential and the anger to succeed.
    Was she capable or was she a true servant of God?
    Even the wolves and crows disobeyed their master.

I recall being thrown deep into the woods.
    I could feel the branches splinter
    And the leaves rub against my skin as I passed.
    My spine against a hardened trunk halted my movement.
    The tree buckled from the fight and tilted to the ground.
    The sweet smell of sap held my senses.
    The wind swayed the trees, as she approached.

On one knee facing down, my head was lifted
    Until my eyes looked upon her.
    Her study began again, but my displeasure for her
    Influenced my next disrespectful deed.

A hand full of dirt filled her eyes prompting my release.
    Her finger wiped her open mouth to rid the substance.
    Her hand trembled and her muscles shifted.
    I saw her think freely, not as a pawn of God,
    But as an individual entity.
    Her mind was racing to control the anger.
    I had tempted her well.
    My death would be her death.
    My failure would be her failure.
    Her face of beauty stained with blood and dirt;
    Her mind pondering my outcome.

I remember her reaching down, grabbing my split chest
    Like it was a basket; using my ribs as the handle.
    The force lifted my torso as my arms to bent backwards.
    As I was being raised, the world seemed to stop.

The Harvester

The leaves no longer floated; the trees no longer swayed.
I could not feel the wind; I could not feel my heart.
The once hidden stars now were clear for all to see.
I have seen the darkest of nights and brightest of days,
But I had never seen the sky distorted before.
Vengeance controlled the reigns
As it drained into the thickened trees.

I do not know if I died that night.
    I do not know if she met the same fate as I,
    But her anger was subdued.
    The clouds converged upon both of us.
    The rest remains darkened and hidden
    Within the surrounding trees.

II: Enlightenment

I wish I could recall everything that happened,
   Not for my understanding,
   But for my appreciation of God's power.

Once again, I awoke in a barely lit cave.
   The candlelight flickered on the rocky ceiling,
   And I felt my right arm being pulled with pressure.
   When my vision adjusted,
   I rotated my head to see Asmodeus smiling.

The vision of my dear demon friend of lust
   Was comforting to me, but it did not last.
   I could not feel my legs; only my left arm.
   I raised my head and saw that my
   Legs were detached from my body,
   But still aligned just below my torso.

My eyes pulsated with panic.
   Asmodeus tried to calm me,
   But the sight of my detached limbs
   Blocked out any hope of pacifying me.
   I swayed my torso, trying to collect the pieces,
   As if merely touching the severed stumps would help.

The Harvester

My friend climbed upon my chest and held my face.
   She hushed my trembling soul
   As my eyes shifted violently within my skull.
   My shaking came under control,
   But my heart and breath remained unstable.
   She caressed my forehead and sang a sweet song.

She said that she was sewing my left arm on
   And that she would get to my legs in due time.
   The pressure I felt from my right arm
   Was from her stitching my flesh back together.

I laid my head back down and stared at the cavern ceiling,
   Trying desperately to forget about my legs,
   While she told me the story as to how she found me.

She said that she was drawn
   To the village by my presence there,
   But when she arrived, I had already been dismembered.
   Her conversation soothed my pounding heart,
   As she had always done in the past.
   Always telling me what I needed to hear.
   I trusted that she would reconstruct my body.

With my limbs being sewn back together,
   I had time to dwell on my situation;
   To reflect upon my reality and task.

Why was my captor visiting?
   The encounters never ended well for me.
   I thought about each visitation.
   They all had one trait in common;
   Depression.

My depression caused me to avoid my task.
   My depression always subdued me,

To the point where I ventured away from my path;
Away from God's plan.

I assumed I was being punished for my betrayal.
    She served as my alternative to fulfilling God's desires.
    She was the shifting winds and ever changing tides,
    Used to steer my ship's sails.
    She was my balance;
    My walking cane upon the path of God.

Asmodeus smiled at my thoughts
    As she finished attaching my right shoulder.
    She described my captor as a banshee of God's will.
    I used both of my arms to prop myself up.
    My friend crouched along the floor
    And slid one of my legs close.
    I felt blood drain into my foot as each vein adjoined.
    Soon I was able to bend my toes.
    Such a small action, but well missed.

Standing upon two legs again,
    I had no revenge planned for the banshee,
    As she was only doing her task.
    However, my new goal was to never see her again.
    If God desired for me to unleash sin onto mankind,
    Then I would fulfill my promise.

Asmodeus collected her belongings.
    We walked from the cave
    And stood on the threshold of the hill
    Overlooking the village below.
    I turned to speak to my friend,
    But she was no longer by my side.
    She was there only when I needed her.
    Nothing more, nothing less.

The Harvester

With no possessions to call my own, I felt reborn.
    The night air tasted different.
    My head was clear of clouds.
    My eyes were no longer blinded.
    My burden was concise with a path laid out.
    No longer obstructed with crossroads.
    No more wonderment; no more confusion.

Before I proceeded along God's way,
    I had unfinished chores within the village.
    I walked past the river,
    Where they drowned me.
    I walked past the column,
    Where they burned and staked me.

In front of the door where the wine flowed
    Was the young child with his branch in hand.
    His persona shifted to be Amon, the demon of wrath.

She handed me two short scythes
    And proceeded to open the door.
    I accepted her gifts as an invitation and walked inside.

All of the villagers who held me captive
    During my weakened state were there.
    I felt my blood boil and my heart race.
    Their eyes widened at my presence.
    They had each taken ownership for my demise
    And used my hallowed torso as evidence
    To secure their stories of personal heroism,
    But they were not heroes.
    They were judging eyes that preyed upon the weak.
    Unfortunate for them, I was no longer weak.

They were each frozen to their chairs at the sight of me.
    Their fears realized, as I locked the door behind me.

Jones

They never could have given me death;
For I was death.

I was everything a man should fear.
    I was the dark of night; the shadow behind the sun.
    I was the demon they took me for,
    But I was much more than that.
    I was something no mortal man could relate to.
    I shared the same flesh and bone, but my core was evil.

In front of the door, I stood.
    On the edge of madness, I resided.
    My breath for the first time matched my beating heart.
    My eyes were closed, but I could see everyone.

The hero of the crowd, the one who covered my face
    With goat flesh, rose from his chair.
    The eyes of his peers were upon him,
    Prompting him to be the hero once more.
    With slight hesitation, he came to me.
    There were so many ways I could have killed him.

With urging shouts from the crowd,
    He reached out with both arms in hopes to grab me.
    He would never touch anything again.
    I rotated my scythes and separated both of his arms.

As he kneeled before me in pain,
    I rested my blades on either side of his neck.
    He pleaded with me, but his words were not heard.
    His tears were not for the remorse of torturing me,
    But for his own salvation.
    His mouth filled with spit and slurred his speech.
    My blades pressed against his throat,
    Denying it the method of swallowing.

The Harvester

With the eyes of the crowd upon me,
 My blades crossed against each other
 Releasing the head from its owner.

Fear struck the room, as they witnessed
 Their only chance for survival slump to the ground.
 I fed on their terror; I drank from their panic.
 Life was not an option for them.

I tore through their flesh.
 I was immune to their pleas.
 My scythes carved through their flesh with ease,
 The blades never becoming dull.
 I had a sense of relief as I stood within a sea of red,
 Blades dripping with the mortal substance.
 With no more confusion or depression,
 I was enlightened by the freedom my mind gifted me.

Two villagers remained untouched by my hand.
 Each trying desperately to keep their distance from me.
 I stood above them as they trembled.
 I wiped one of my blades on his clothes
 Before carving seven slits into his forehead.
 One for every day I spent in that cave.
 For every demon I met; for every sin I endured.
 Seven.

I flipped the other over and ripped apart his shirt.
 His bare chest served as a canvas for my name.
 I carved deep so that regardless of the healing process,
 The letters of my name would be scarred.
 Satan.

They would each live to tell the tale;
 Forced to travel in separate directions,
 Never overstaying within a village, town or city.

Their stories would relive my visit;
Their scars would be their backing.
Burdened to spread the story of what happened.

I had promised God upon leaving the cave,
    That all would know my name.
    And it would happen, one village at a time.
    I unlocked the door to allow the two survivors outside.
    I could hear their screams as they ran.

My stay within the village had been too long winded;
    I had other relationships to forge.
    I headed north with the stars as my guide.

After a long period of isolated travel, I heard a familiar sound.
    The faint tone of squeaking wheels greeted me.
    Leviathan, the demon of envy was approaching.
    A large grin on his face greeted me,
    And he immediately began
    One of his traditional, everlasting conversations.

Although not my first choice for companionship,
    I was still grateful for him to join me.
    As we walked, he mostly talked.

We spoke of my meetings with Amon and Asmodeus.
    He informed me they would appear to me when needed;
    That they were an extension of me.
    I was their leader
    And connected beyond ways I would not understand.
    For now, my conscious held that power.
    When I got angry, Amon would appear to guide me.
    When my pride surfaced, Lucifer would emerge.
    He said that the concept goes deeper than that though.
    My mind would decipher which demon to summon.
    Traits of sloth, did not always mean Belphegor

Would be the demon of choice.
My fate, my journey would be kept straight and narrow;
My demons were my guide to drag me along.

He said as my gifts matured,
    I would be able to beckon who I choose.
    But for now, I was at the mercy of my mind.

I asked him about the banshee who haunted my dreams.
    I asked if there were others.
    He said each banshee is granted just one person.
    Mine was unique only to me;
    Built from my darkest imagination.

He explained that the banshee
    Was one of the many eyes of God.
    A scout upon land that researches her prey
    And sends word back to her master.

Regardless of the topics at hand,
    Levi did help pass the time,
    We soon neared a boundary gate
    With a sign that read 'City of Hell.'
    I turned to ask Levi a question, but he had disappeared.
    He had served his purpose and departed.
    I was quickly approached by a person asking me
    What purpose I had in the city.

My silence prompted him
    To ask if I was part of the trading caravan.
    My response was *yes*.
    Laughter and celebration created the aroma of the city.
    Everyone's face consisted of wide-eyed expressions.
    They all freely roamed, some even dancing.
    So much happiness made for quite a peculiar sensation.

Jones

I walked along the main path receiving smiles
    And colliding with apologetic people.
    Every eye contact was followed by a greeting.
    It was a social celebration of life,
    Where all rejoiced in the gifts they had received.

Some handed out flowers while others shared drink.
    The amount of serenity I had witnessed
    Was enough for me to wish
    I had never walked through the gate.

After a few more wonderful meetings,
    I grew anxious.
    An adjacent shadow enclave called to me
    And offered isolation from the crowds.
    Within the shadows, I exhaled deeply.
    I was grateful to be hidden from the sun;
    The light meant more smiles and happiness.
    If not for the hidden haze and the pause it gave me,
    The city would have had nothing to smile about.

With my nerves calming and my skin embattled,
    I studied my surroundings and found a small corridor.
    The darkness leading downward fed my curiosity.
    In such a bright celebratory city,
    A tunnel of black was a blessing.
    No cheering, no dancing, no laughter.
    Only a dark, damp and cold wooden door.
    The escaping cool breeze filled my lungs with acceptance.

Darkness was the first welcoming from the city
    That I actually accepted.
    Narrow stone stairs supplied a pathway
    For my descent and led me into a large cavern.
    Streaks of sunlight gleamed through the cracks,
    But were devoured by the shades of grey.

The Harvester

A flowing stream separated the cavern floor in half
And provided a beautiful sound.

Disregarded by the city, the cavern was abandoned
And hidden behind the shadows.
All who frolicked in the sun and warmth of others,
Would find no such pleasures under city.

That was where I found my serenity.
My acceptance was gifted by the shadows.
My security was granted by the hidden sanctuary.

During my appreciation of my new dwelling,
Lucifer appeared before me.
His long yellow hair and beard split the darkness.
It made sense for him to appear;
Pride had filled my heart at that moment.
He greeted me with honor and respect,
I showed the same in return.

We talked of the path of God.
He spoke of hidden sources deep within my mind.
Mastering the traits would assist me in my task.
I was to practice my skills during my stay in the city.
His words of corruption and defiance would be a gift.

He praised my wrath in the previous village
But acknowledged the small effort.
I had to grow in my intentions, expand my horizons.
My path brought me to the city of Hell
And releasing my abilities would allow me to leave.

After Lucifer left, I sat on the banks of the stream,
Listening to my thoughts.

Jones

I do not understand how I was able to achieve
    What I am about to discuss next, but the knowledge
    Would serve as a turning point in my studies.

I lifted an arm to stretch my shoulder.
    As I did, a large stone rose into the air.
    I lowered my arm and the stone followed.
    I rested my arm and the stone fell to the ground.
    Again, I focused on the stone, raising it off the ground.
    I pulled it closer and then pushed it away.
    With a quick sway of my palm,
    The stone shattered against the wall.

I focused on the running stream.
    The cool, clear water became turbulent.
    I smiled at the idea of controlling elements.
    After my discovery, I ventured back to the upper city.
    The sun was bright exiting into the corridor.
    My anxiety grew, and I shielded my eyes.
    The sounds of another festival echoed through my ears.

People were dancing and singing.
    Rose petals covered the street;
    Green leaves were being tossed in excitement.
    If there was ever a city that needed corruption,
    It was Hell.

As the sun disappeared behind the city walls,
    All of the citizens migrated inside.
    They did so in a quick manner,
    As if they were afraid of the dark.
    The night received no celebration,
    No festival for the stars.
    It was only me alone in the street,
    With an entire city within my grasp.

The Harvester

I wanted to start small in my quest,
    So I slaughtered a few of their cattle
    And displayed the corpses in an upright position.
    Their hooves submerged in a thick pool of blood.

Some might find the sight disturbing,
    But I found it to be the most beautiful vision
    I had seen in the city since arriving.
    Back down I went for some much needed rest.
    I slept to the sounds of the cow blood
    Dripping through the cracks, down into the stream.

I awoke to the aroma of rotting flesh,
    But also to the sounds of more celebration.
    My confusion led me up to the city,
    Where I witnessed more dancing and singing.
    They were celebrating life through the death of the cows.
    Somehow I had provided another reason for a festival.
    Frustration fed my emotions.

My wrath spiked at the sight, but instead of Amon,
    I saw Beelzebub, the demon of gluttony,
    Dancing across the street.
    He broke rhythm and made his way through the crowd.

He said he couldn't help himself from partaking.
    I was not as amused as he.
    It was good that Amon did not appear,
    As I would have followed my rage
    And murdered the entire population.

Beelzebub calmed me with his words.
    He spoke about how greed could work.
    But my mind was in too much turmoil to listen.
    Merging back into the crowd, Beelzebub disappeared.
    I needed something more dramatic than cows

Jones

To rattle the emotions of the city.
Their happiness was strong, but my will was stronger.

With that resolve, I grabbed the nearest person
And swiftly pulled him down into my dwelling.
The speed of the force blackened his vision.

When he awoke, he was lying on his back.
Each of his limbs were tied to boulders,
His body soaking in the current.
He looked around franticly,
As if he was searching for answers;
I knew he would find none.

His entire life up until that point was happiness.
I doubted that the understanding would ever reach him,
But watching him struggle for reason was enjoyable.
It felt as if I was watching myself;
Through the struggles I once lived through in that cave.
The confusion, the torment; all without understanding.

The city seemed to believe that man could do no wrong.
So, even while being bound within water,
He greeted me as if I was to release him.
He said he was having difficulties removing his hands.
Was it possible that his emotions
Were so deeply trained that no fear even existed?

Soon he smiled uncontrollably.
A blessing in my eyes, as I saw an opportunity;
A flaw in the happiness.
I said no words;
Only observed his downward spiral of emotions.

Once he knew that I was not going to rescue him,
His facial expressions altered.

The Harvester

Fear was what I desired.
How deep would his thoughts go?
Moments earlier, he was dancing in the sunlight,
Now he struggled in the darkness, confused.

His anxiousness turned to a fight for freedom.
    True fear always led to violent acts;
    The binds tore into his wrists
    With every twist and turn for release.

I had to remind myself that the thoughts of sin
    I endured within my imprisonment
    Did not exist within this world.
    He truly knew nothing of sin or evil,
    Therefore did not know how to react.
    In his mind, I was suppose to help him.
    That was what any other person would have done.
    Why should the expectation of me be any different?
    His confusion was not from fear,
    But from that notion that I had not freed him.

I felt pity for his sheltered mind: I could relate.
    I was once like him when I was back on my farm.
    Fear of the unknown did not exist for me then.
    Upon my own land, I was a king.

But unlike him, I had now seen the horror of the world.
    I had seen the corruption of man
    Through the murderous ways of others.
    Life was not song and flowers.
    Life was a balance between day and night;
    One more wholesome than the other.

As the water crested his chest,
    He still looked to me for release.
    As the water filled his ears,

Jones

He extended his neck to conquer the rise.
After a final inhale, he sealed his lips.
His eyes were wide open;
His head trembled in a panic.
Soon, his body absorbed the safety reservoir of air.
His mouth opened, and the water seeped inside.
His body grew lifeless, except for twitches.
I was indebted to him; his death provided knowledge
Regarding a mind full of serenity.

I was above ground early, long before the rise of the sun.
  I perched his body on the stone,
  The center of the festivities.
  It was a sacred monument of sorts.
  How would they react to a corpse tied to their relic?
  I viewed the scene as art,
  My second welcoming gift to the city of Hell.

As the sun rose to an intolerable level,
  Out emerged the residents of the city.
  There was no dancing, no celebrating.
  All that was replaced with tears of sorrow.
  Death slapped each of them across the face
  As they stared at the bloated corpse.

I did not desire screams or chaos,
  I only wanted the concept of fear
  To blend with their fictitious views of the world.
  I needed their acceptance that evilness
  Existed within the land
  And that their city was not immune to it.

The word spread throughout the city
  And even to the hilltop palace of the king.
  Within moments, the happy king
  Headed down the street accompanied

The Harvester

By his loyal companions to see for himself.
To the population,
The king represented safety and solidarity.
To me, he represented an opportunity
To expand my gift giving.

I looked upon their beaten faces
While waiting for the king to arrive.
Never had they felt such despair.
Most just roamed aimlessly with no purpose.
The disruption in their peaceful pattern
Had shattered the very meaning of their lives.

The only celebration was buried deep within my mind
Where I and my fellow demons
Paraded the corpse through the streets.
We tossed blood and fragments of flesh
Instead of flowers and bread.
We sang hymns of destruction and violence
Instead of nature and love.
Our dark parade would last forever within our dreams.

The king ordered the cleansing of the fountain.
I peered around the crowd to capture a sinful gesture.
I wanted anger to emerge from the skin
Of just one citizen within the vast majority.
I needed someone to demand punishment
For whoever committed the evilness.
Did they believe it was an act of God?
All of the eyes were filled with tears of sadness.
All of the mouths were filled with words of despair.

Through the moans of sorrow, I found him.
A frail man, near the king, who shed no remorse.
He was the only one not reacting to the scene,
And he seemed to care more about the others.

Jones

Whereas some might view him as disrespectful,
I saw him as an opportunity;
A pawn to extend the reach to the king.

As I watched them walk back to the palace,
I pondered several outcomes,
But the appearance of Mammon shifted my thoughts.
Greed would be the answer.
A king without greed seemed unworthy of his crown;
Power and sin were almost a natural companionship.

To corrupt an entire city,
I needed to corrupt the very entity
That all of the citizens admired.
I needed the king.

As the days passed and the festivals returned,
I was hidden within the shadows,
Far from the eyes of the city,
Undisturbed by the citizens.

The courtyard went back to its original state.
The corpse was all disposed of in an ethical manner
And of course, a celebration was in order.
Although the days were overflowing with joy,
There was a sense of remembrance;
A sense of doubt regarding the world
Beyond the peace loving walls of the city.
There was a hesitation to begin the festivals.
There was a silence before each song.
The atmosphere was changing as questions lingered.
The doubt of all being good haunted them.

As silence and night fell upon the buildings,
I emerged from my dwelling with Mammon by my side.
We ventured up the windy road to the hilltop palace.

The Harvester

In a place with no fear or hatred,
There was no need for guards.

As the advisor to the king slept,
　　Mammon and I visited him.
　　Through the whispering of our voices,
　　We attacked his dreams.
　　We decayed his fantasies and destroyed his passions.
　　His muscles began to twitch as we continued.

We spoke of the benefits of greed and the prosperity of sin.
　　We spoke of opportunity and commitment.
　　With our vision embedded in the skull of the advisor,
　　We walked from the palace.

Questions plagued my mind that night.
　　How much would the advisor believe?
　　How much would he follow his dreams?
　　The approaching morning would carry the answers
　　Like the aroma of flowers through the wind.
　　For once, I welcomed the sun.

As the city celebrated another festival
　　Regarding something I did not understand,
　　I saw the advisor walking toward the courtyard.
　　He silenced the crowd with scroll in his hand.

His announcement was that the king
　　Had decided to tax the festivals.
　　In order to participate in the celebrations,
　　One would first contribute coin.
　　I paid close attention and saw resentment
　　Flood the audience like a raging river.
　　Confusion and astonishment coated the people's faces.

Jones

My whisper of greed was well perceived by the advisor
    And even more accepted by the king.
    More wealth, more power.
    A combination that any good king
    Would be foolish to ignore.

The anguish of the city increased
    As people chose not to accept the king's demands.
    My voice through the corridors encircled the residents
    Like a snake inflicting them with venom in their ears.
    The vision of the once great king
    Deteriorated into a vast pool of greed.
    Anger and bitterness clouded the skies,
    Blocking the happiness of the sun.
    My nightly rituals of visiting the advisor in his sleep
    Kept the situation alive and fresh.

The next morning, the advisor announced that the king
    Would also accept gifts as payments for celebrating.
    The emotions erupted from displeasure to anger;
    A level which only offered me even more options.

Anger, rage and hatred were a recipe for complete disorder.
    Once achieved, the mind could be manipulated.
    An angry mind
    Had enough pain to shadow any rational thought;
    Laying down all guard so that infection could proceed.

The crowd shouted back at the advisor.
    They wanted freedom, they wanted justice.
    I would be the one to offer them both.

Their eyes widened as my voice traveled,
    Floating though the crowds like anaroma.
    I whispered thoughts of marching to the palace.
    Anger, a beautiful aspect of humans.

The Harvester

It seizes up the mortal mind,
Completely closing the gates to rational thought.

If any such catalyst was needed for sin,
    The emotion of anger was the key.
    Just days before, the city was celebrating life,
    Now they were storming the palace.

I was warming up to the city.
    I began to admire the architecture and landscape.
    The way the corridors shadowed themselves
    Was a beauty to behold.
    The stone structures and paths were not meant
    To support such happiness.

As the mindless, angry mob
    Walked up to the unguarded palace door,
    I had a moment of pride,
    Prompting Lucifer to appear again.
    He spoke of the longevity of sin.
    His words reduced my acceptance,
    But also enlightened me with additional visions.
    Consistency in sin needed to be fluid.
    If their anger was left untouched,
    Their minds would have an opportunity
    To regain control; destroying the work.

A lapse in the mind meant an alternate choice.
    An alternate path meant rationalizing the situation;
    Therefore emotions would become untangled.

I quickly ran amongst the group,
    Making my way to the doors.
    With my fists, I pounded on the wood.
    The anger in the crowd returned and intensified
    As more fists joined my own.
    The redness of their visions was saved,

But they needed help to advance to the next phase:
Violence.
They were not capable of progressing on their own,
As sin was still new to their abilities.

With a swift kick,
    I was able to splinter the wood.
    The mass of people pushed through the blockade
    And entered into the main area of the palace.
    They were greeted by the king and his advisor.

As much as I had whispered into the ears of the mob,
    I had also said as much to the king and his pawn.
    To counteract my own idea,
    I had informed the advisor to take up arms
    In case such a situation would arise.
    Behind the king stood several armed guards.
    The weapons were new to such a peaceful city.
    Constructed by the tormented mind of one king.

Before me stood quite a unique situation.
    One where both parties could gain and lose.
    The scales were balanced with silence.
    One palm held the rebellious nature of the citizens,
    Whereas the other held the ruling head of the king.

No more whispers were gifted to the ears;
    No more visions of deception were presented.
    My task was complete.
    All that remained was for one person to act;
    To follow through with the means.

I did not care who would be the victor.
    Any potential outcome would suffice,
    Unless they chose to have a festival
    To celebrate their indifferences.

The Harvester

I found my medium in a peasant man.
    His frown was deeply engraved within his skin
    With no signs of relinquishing his disgust for the king.
    He had accepted my sinful ways as the only path.

His soul, his essence, his well-being were now mine.
    I waited patiently for him to step forward.
    After hateful words continued to leak from his mouth,
    He spat on the king.

The guards tightened their grips on their weapons.
    With a mere signal from his wrist,
    The king ordered the slaughter to commence.
    Blood spilled, staining the pristine floors
    Of the once peaceful and welcoming entryway.
    My attention was on the king.
    I watched his every gesture as the citizens
    Were being butchered like infected pigs.
    No sorrow, no remorse, reflected in his eyes.
    Only pure, raw despise flowed through his veins.
    He was now a servant of my doing,
    Fulfilling my every need and desire.

While the guards were determining
    Who amongst the dead were still alive,
    Sunlight and the curious eyes from those outside
    Overwhelmed the dead room.

The king ordered his guards to block the entrance,
    But the vision of death quickly spread amongst the city.
    Soon, every person would know
    What the king had done on that day.

The insanity that filled the streets and corridors
    On the days to follow was much to my liking.
    Chants of hatred sang through the air

And rose above the city like a hovering cloud.
The wind carried the torments of the people
High into the stone inlets of the palace
Where the ears of the king could not find shelter.

Sleep deprived and enraged by the citizens,
The king called forth his advisor.
My plan lived deep within the mind of his ally.
My visit to him the previous night was a successful one.

He informed the king to meet the anger with an iron fist.
A disrespectful citizen could corrupt many.
Any night could see another attack on the palace.

As the sun rose the next day, the people of Hell were greeted
With new laws posted on every wall.
Resentment toward the king was not acceptable;
Punishable by death.
When threatened with their demise,
Humans will cower to save their pitiful existence.
They will shield their voices to appease the king's ruling.

Death was not something the citizens should have feared;
There were much more horrific situations in life.
Regardless, the human instinct was to flee
To avoid any contact with the king or his guards.

Regardless of how far they ran,
My whispers were still being delivered by the wind.
Every night, every wakening day, the songs were being sung.
I made sure the king heard every hymn.

The constant bombardment of resentment
Was enough to push any rational person to insanity.
Several rises of the moon was all the king needed.

The Harvester

With the advisor backing his notions,
    The king unleashed pain upon the city.
    His reign of fear,
    Brought about by fictitious whispers of denial,
    Devastated the very foundation of his ruling.

The road to the hilltop palace was closed;
    The courtyard became bare.
    The fountain decayed; the city became dead.
    Public beatings were held daily
    So that everyone knew the consequences
    For not obeying the laws.

The sun would never shine as bright again.
    The wind would never feel the same.
    A grey hue tinted the clouds,
    Threatening with unpredictable storms.

The shadows were abundant;
    The darkness was sheer black.
    As I roamed the streets alone,
    I became somewhat attached to Hell.
    Over time, the city had altered into a decent place.

I was not alone in my nightly rituals;
    Guards often patrolled the corridors in search of victims
    To sacrifice for the good of the law.

With no one else available, I was an obvious choice.
    The mortal mind was a curious relic.
    If they knew my name, would they continue their quest?
    Would they approach me,
    Knowing that I could end their lives
    With one gaze into my eyes?

Jones

As the guards approached,
    I knew the answer to my questions.
    To them, I was nothing.
    To the king, I was an example.
    To me, the shift toward my direction
    Ended their well-being.

They encircled me with their armor and spears.
    We danced in the corridor that night.
    I pondered death for each of them.
    My scythes were concealed beneath my cloak,
    But seemed too easy a path for me to take.
    I randomly chose one of the guards to focus on.

With my thoughts swirling,
    Levi appeared on the back of the guard
    And whispered a sweet sin deep into his ear.
    I do not know the exact message,
    But the guard's demeanor altered.
    Levi vanished as quickly as he had appeared,
    Leaving behind a sinful infection within the guard.

I saw the hesitation;
    The pattern I had grown to admire and love.
    While his comrade looked to me, he did not.

With a heavy grip around the shaft of his spear,
    He buried the tip into the neck of his companion.
    The blade split the flesh and protruded to the other side.
    The force tilted the large helmet.

To retrieve his weapon,
    The guard placed a heavy boot on the torso.
    The sound of tearing flesh against metal appeased me,
    But it did not phase the other guards.

The Harvester

All spears rotated from me
    And pointed in the direction of the altered guard.
    Levi never told me what exactly he whispered,
    But it was enough to condemn the man.

With a forward attack,
    The guard plunged his spear into the other's stomach.
    The victim coughed, vomited
    And spit blood all over his polished chest armor.

Instead of pulling the spear out,
    The guard pushed the shaft deeper
    Into the flesh until it was reachable from behind.
    He grabbed the wood,
    Pulling the rest of his weapon through.

There has always been a strange beauty about sin.
    The passion, the unknowing with regards to the actions
    That the human mind could create.
    With a mere whisper, a mortal mind can be tormented
    To the edge where God no longer exists.

That night, I pondered whether
    There were humans in the world
    Who would *not* need persuasion.
    I longed for the day to greet those who desired
    Nothing from me to provoke sin;
    True disciples of my passion.

While in personal thought,
    I had missed the encounter with the third guard.
    However, I saw the victim's head slanted backwards,
    Looking up to the stars, swallowing his own spear.
    With his eyes and mouth agape,
    Nothing but the shaft extended beyond his lips.
    His lifeless legs curled beneath him,

Jones

The spear kept his upper body ridged,
Providing him with a second spine.
His lungs choked on blood.

The fourth guard ran toward the palace.
Alone I stood with the sinful guard.
As he pointed his spear toward me,
I ended his life quickly with the rotation of his neck.
Leaving the corpses of the guards within the courtyard,
I ventured back through the corridor.

The troubled creek in my underground abode
Awakened me with the sound of its current.
Commotion spilled down through the crevices
And prompted me to stretch my aching bones.

Out in the courtyard remained the deceased guards,
Decaying slowly in the morning sun.
The stench of their rotting corpses
Leaked through their armored casings.
A large group of citizens surrounded them
To the point where others could not easily witness.

Observing the commotion, a change occurred in me.
I wanted it all; the palace, the courtyard, the corridors.
The city would serve as my realm;
The palace shall serve as my home.
It would prove to be no easy task to capture the city.
My pride for Hell conjured Lucifer to guide me.
Although he requested that I not proceed,
He eventually had no choice but to relinquish.
I wasn't sure whether my mind was tormenting me,
But the determination of acquiring the city remained.
Every piece of the wall, every shadow, every stone.

The Harvester

The city would be mine . . . but how?
I found the answer within my haven.
I could not imagine my kingdom upon God's land
Where the living could roam as they pleased.
The mere thought clenched my muscles.
The sun shining brightly every day did not appease me.
I desired the city with every essence of my being,
Just not in the same area where it currently resided.
The distance from Heaven, the observance of the stars.

The next day, outside the gates,
I walked the perimeter of the city encircling the land,
Allowing my scythe to trail behind me,
Its blade dredging deep into the earth.
I dragged my weapon, carving into God's terrain.
The land did not care for my disobedience;
The once soft soil turned to stone,
But the sharpness of my blade backed by my strength
Allowed me to continue.

Along the ground-butchering way,
Each of my fellow demons appeared
In a failed attempt to persuade me otherwise.
They called me mad, but I knew my mind was clear.

I believed God intended to halt my movement.
Mountains appeared where there previously were none.
Vast lakes consumed the land, but still I walked.

Ravenous wolves tried to block my path.
I dealt with them and stepped over their dead carcasses
As I reinserted my blade back into the earth.

Wild boars awaited me with blood stained,
Sharpened tusks protruding from their snarling lips.
I removed the tusks of one

And used them to slaughter the others,
Then continued on my way.

The atmosphere became disgusted with me.
    The skies vomited on the land with shards of ice.
    Lightning galloped across the skies with vengeance.

My deed was complete.
    All that remained was the understanding from the sky.
    Instead, a thunderous growl uprooted nearby trees
    And tossed them aside as if they were weak branches.
    The mountains trembled while the sun vanished.
    I had never seen the sky blackened
    To the point where the clouds cried.
    The ice tore at my flesh, but I stood in acceptance.
    The lightning pulled at my skin,
    But I stood in acceptance.
    The rain fell heavy.
    No mortal would dare stand beneath the sky.
    They sought shelter quickly and wisely.
    Even my demons fled, but not me.
    As new lakes and canyons were formed
    I stood outside the city wall and placed both hands
    On the stone in hopes to ease the trembling.
    I only wanted the structure of the city.
    I held onto the wall as the earth began to quake.
    I felt myself rise and fall with the land,
    But still I held onto the wall.

As the sky tired and calmed,
    My flesh was torn to the bone, but I remained alive.
    I believed in my decision and carried my scythe
    Back through the gates of the city.

The citizens returned outside
    And guards led the king to the courtyard

The Harvester

By parting the crowd with their spears.
Astonishment coated the king's face
As the vision of the deceased guards filled his eyes.
Without assistance from his mind,
He accused the rebellious citizens of murder.

Panic erupted in the courtyard, much to my pleasure.
    The innocent tried to flee,
    But they were met with the guard's weapons.
    Cloth was torn, flesh was ripped;
    All at the king's demands.
    More guards blocked the exiting corridors
    So that no one could escape.
    The eyes of the king met with mine.
    With a signal of his hand,
    Several guards advanced on me.

Each hand that touched me, left its owner.
    Screams of agony funneled through their armor.
    I walked back into the courtyard,
    Where the displeased king ordered more death.

I was surrounded by more guards,
    But kept my thoughts fixated upon the king.
    His trustworthy advisor stood by his side.
    I whispered to the advisor as he spoke to the king.
    End the citizen's life was the order.

A rise of the king's hand sent more guards.
    However, I opted for a choice other than a swift death.
    One, I assumed, that only God had foreseen.
    The reason behind the anger of the skies.
    The reason behind the warnings from my demons.
    The reason why I encircled the city.

Jones

I raised my arm and with a mighty fist,
    Dove my hand deep into the foundation of the city.
    The power shook the buildings, stumbling the guards.
    The act sent five large cracks filtering through the city
    Connecting with my outer engraved circle.

The ground trembled with violence
    As the city began to sink.
    Everyone who remained, struggled to stay upright.
    They looked for understanding,
    But they would receive nothing except fear
    As the city was consumed by the earth.

I rode my newly acquired relic down into the pit
    As the sun slowly disappeared from sight.
    I reveled in the screams that greeted the darkness.
    As the plummet came to a halt,
    Those not weighed by armor
    Found themselves floating above the city.
    Their cries were silenced
    As their bodies reunited with the land
    In piles of broken bones and flesh.

With a rise of my hand, the dead citizens of the city rose.
    Blood soaked and bruised, I fed their minds
    With new life and comfort to ease their confusion.

I chose two of the king's guards
    And burdened them with guarding the gates of Hell.
    Pale in skin, the guards rose and accepted their fate.

I requested seven live citizens to remain untouched.
    Each were brought before me
    And granted safe passage back to the upper world.
    Their task was to spread the tale
    Of what happened on that day.

The Harvester

To ensure they stayed true to their course,
I again carved my name into their chests,
Along with seven marks upon their foreheads.
Once branded, they were free to leave.

The king and his advisor knelt before me
    With wavering hands and mumbled speech.
    They had accepted sin with such ease
    That I finally determined they should duel.
    Each was given a dagger.
    The victor would receive a place on my council,
    While the other would become a servant.

Their human minds no longer struggled with death.
    Fear encased their visions and blurred their thoughts.

Uncertainty plagues the mortal mind.
    One should accept the idealism of the unknown.
    I waited for one of them to embrace the challenge
    And understand the concept that life
    Was an insignificant portion of their existence.
    A clinch in the jaw of the advisor was evident enough.
    A lunge forward allowed for the blade
    To enter the king's stomach.
    My council had its first member
    And I had my first servant.

III: Production

Within my new city,
Torches aligned the corridors and courtyard
To provide passageway through the blackness.
The dead roamed without purpose,
But eventually found tasks that needed completion.
The stench of living flesh was removed
And replaced with an aura of damnation.

Every essence of the former king was dispelled.
Every celebratory element of the city was torched.
Every flag was buried deep within the ground.
My underground sanctuary was left unchanged
And was forbidden to all who dwelled within the realm.

The most pressing matter about my new kingdom
Was the dead that seemed to arrive daily.
At first I was shocked by the appearance of so many.
I had no idea if it was God's will or my own doing.
Either way, I had to deal with the dead.

All mortal minds are born with a simple gift from God;
His idealism, a complete understanding of his presence.
My burden was to cloud that existence
Through sinful encounters.

The Harvester

My demons and I sought out hesitations toward God.
And those arriving at my gates
Had obviously fallen for my temptation in some way

Hidden deep within the earth,
    Far from the eyes of the sun,
    The city was becoming a realm of prosperity.
    From the trenches of the land,
    The condemned ones found their way to my haven.
    Their punishment would vary
    Depending on their overall acceptance of sin.
    Although all fates would prove unfavorable.

My fellow demons were hesitant
    To show appreciation for the city
    And the constantly overpopulated dead.
    I could not dwell within their emotions,
    As there was much work to be done.
    They would have my ear,
    Just not at that present time.

⁂

Warnings sent through the wind flowed through Hell,
    Speaking of God's displeasure.
    The cavern ceiling would often tremble,
    Sending large boulders to the buildings below.

Stealing an entire city from the land of God
    Was an unruly punishable offense,
    But necessary for my vision.
    I was not about to construct a new city
    When Hell accommodated me
    And offered me a sanctuary.
    I did not consider myself a rebel,
    Nor did I take a different path away from my task.

Jones

I desired a dwelling to conduct my ventures.
I did not view it as greed to take a city
So corrupt in atmosphere and dead in population.

However, God apparently did not hold a similar view.
His wrath still lingered within my mind,
Knowing that he could strike unannounced.
I would not have to wait long, as a low hymn
Echoed through the caverns
And danced with the flames of the torches.

An evil breeze snaked through the corridors
And shivered the souls of those unfortunate to hear.
The city stalled and froze beneath the sound of silence.
My heart sank deep into my chest.
She was here within my cavern; within my realm.

I walked to the gates and greeted the guards.
Their skin shook beneath their armor.
Their presence remained strong,
But their souls struggled internally.
I stepped between them
And gazed upon the large field leading to the city.
Nothing but the sound of song existed.
However, I knew that when there was a hymn,
Pain was not far behind.

In the horizon, she appeared.
From what I could decipher, she was in her hag form,
Wobbling along the path with the help of a cane.

Her song grew louder as she neared.
Slowly she crept, her cane stabbing the land.
My mouth moistened;
My heart pounded, rattling my rib cage.

The Harvester

I was forced to wait
    And could do nothing but anticipate.
    What fate did she carry? What fear did she bring?

Her hood concealed her eyes.
    Her white, straggly hair extended past her rotten teeth.
    Her hand held tightly to her cane to push her along.
    Options streamed through my mind,
    But none would match her strength and hatred for me.
    God's servant could not be reasoned with;
    God's servant could not shed pity.

She was close; I could smell her stench of death.
    Her eyes remained hidden as she walked passed me.
    The guards gripped their spears as she approached.
    That small gesture of misunderstanding halted her.
    Her hood turned slightly to gaze upon the guards.
    Their armor hid the suffering of their lifeless bodies.
    Twisting sounds of flesh leaked through the metal.
    Crackling bones distorted the wind.
    The structures of their armor remained intact,
    But only God knew the kind of devastation
    That was occurring within their casings.

As the guards crumpled to the ground,
    She walked through the gates.
    No attention was given to me.
    One step into the city, she stopped.
    Her hood rotating from side to side.
    Her eyes of God surveying my abode.

She held up one hand and quickly
    Pulled a hidden citizen from a nearby corridor.
    His dead soul rotated with a sway of her fingers.
    As quickly as he was entrapped,
    He was released back into the corridor.

Jones

She turned to me as I braced for her onslaught.
Her wobbly arm raised; pointing her cane at me.
The tip touched my chest, hovering over my heart.
The idea of being skewered entered my mind
And sent panic through my veins.
I shut my eyes in hopes of
Helping me deal with my approaching demise.
Instead, I felt the wooden cane unlatch from my heart
And return to its support role.

I stared at her shadowed face for any understanding,
 But found nothing.
 She turned and wobbled back through the gates.

With her visit, God knew everything.
 My plans, my visions, my hopes.
 She had scouted my realm,
 Not to destroy it,
 But for the knowledge of the meaning.

Her visions would be returned to God.
 Her song began again, while she walked along the path
 Leading away from the city.
 I, of course, would need more guards.

I wondered what God thought.
 Was I fulfilling his plan? Was I progressing in my task?
 I considered the non-violent meeting
 With the banshee as acceptance.

Instead of dwelling in the unknown,
 I began to enhance the city in particular ways.
 I aligned the entrance to my realm with human skulls;
 The cobbled, uneven path was to my liking.

The Harvester

While admiring my work, I noticed a lone crimson goat.
The hooves were clashing against the bones.

The color of red about him was not a natural hue;
    The animal was soaked in blood.
    My hand slid along its body in search for a wound.
I found none.

Another goat arrived, blood stained like the other.
    I looked to the horizon as more goats appeared.
    My confusion was interrupted
    By small droplets landing upon my shoulder.
    The red substance tempted my eyes to look upward
    Where I witnessed a situation so profound
That I lost all rational thought.

The cracks in the cavern ceiling were leaking blood.
    A sea of red rained down upon me.
    The sadistic storm coated the city in a blanket.

The blood began to pool within the dirt and rise.
    Puddles aligned the corridors and found
    Their way into my underground sanctuary.
    Underneath, I saw my creek being fed by the source.
    The current was agitated, lifting heavy stones.
    The blending of the water and blood was empowering
    As it carved its way downward.
    The shifting sliced through the foundation
    And fractured the land forming a deep trench.
    The earth shook, swaying the city.

I ran through the corridor and out the gates.
    Each pebble, each rock of my realm shuddered.
    A huge crevice forged its way in both directions
    As far as I could see through the rain.

Jones

The rain of blood did not subside.
    The downpour bombarded my cavern,
    With every pool creeping its way into the crevice.
    The city had become stained with crimson.
    All were drenched in the demented rain;
    All were discolored with a wash of death.

On the seventh day, the rain subsided.
    The storm left behind a wide river of red
    With a shifting tide that gifted fear in return.

After the storm subsided,
    I noticed a vast amount of goat carcasses littering the path.
    I followed the corpses until I was led back up to God's land.
    What I saw saddened me.
    What I saw altered my mindset.
    Lying on the the land that once supported the city,
    A pile of rotting goats resided, stretching to the clouds.
    Each slaughtered and drained.
    Still coated in their blood, I stood in awe at the sight.
    No one but God could have achieved such a feat.
    I took land from him.
    In return, he took the only animal that I admired.

As I gazed, the earth shook once more.
    The five cracks that I had created to swallow the city
    Reopened, allowing the pile of goats to plummet.
    The vast mass of carcasses slowly filtered
    Through the ground and rained down upon my realm.
    I looked to the Heavens as the last goat vanished
    And the earth reformed to conceal the crevices.
    I stood coated with the blood from all of earth's goats,
    Knowing that their carcasses had taken over my city.
    I could only offer God a smile.

The Harvester

My cobbled path, my palace, my courtyard
 Were all concealed by the carcasses.
 Destruction of my wall and gates was apparent.
 I had no other option, but to set my city ablaze.
 Knowing that the basic stone structure
 And formation of the walls would survive,
 I threw torches into the mountain of goat
 And watched as the fire leaped from carcass to carcass.
 The inferno spread rapidly,
 Leaving behind molten skeletons.
 The cavern became a slave to the heat.
 For seven more days, the city burned
 As the flesh was devoured by the flame.
 At the end, a sea horned skulls besieged the cavern.
 The stone underpinning of the city remained,
 But was altered to a blackened, red grime.
 I collected all of the goat's skulls before they became
 Embedded within the thick substance.
 The spines were used to align the top of my city wall.
 All other remaining bones of the goats
 Became a part of the outer wall.

The river of goat's blood
 Had grown in size, carving its own trench.
 It was alive with a passion of its own.
 The turbulent river flowed in unpredictable patterns.
 With the rise of the moon, the tides mourned.
 With the rise of the sun, the tides bled crimson.
 Much like a servant in need of its master,
 The river needed to be controlled.
 I had witnessed both its devastation and beauty.
 All of the wandering souls feared the river.
 They trembled if they were near.

To understand the relationship
 Between the dead and river,

Jones

I brought a lone soul to the shoreline.
He was reluctant to travel with me, but a solid grip
Allowed for my companion to follow.

I had seen fear before; I had lived through it.
    I had seen the human mind scar and bend from fear,
    But I had never seen fear
    That intense within a condemned soul.
    I stopped momentarily, my arms shaking
    As if I was holding a wild beast.
    If the soul still had bones,
    He would have broken them.
    If the soul still had flesh,
    The shackles would have carved him.
    Instead, he merely shook violently in my grasp.

I proceeded to drag him to the shoreline
    Where the river could hear us; where it could smell us.
    The current churned with excitement.

The river flowed higher in anticipation
    With every approaching step we took.
    The waves crashed against the rocks
    With a power that would shatter all except God's hands.

It was relentless in its effort to obtain its goal.
    However, it was not the soul it clamored for.
    My flesh was the prize.
    The swell moved as I moved.
    To test my theory, I staked a soul to the river's edge
    Close enough for the beastly river to consume him.
    I walked to an adjacent inlet aligned with jagged rocks
    At a peak that the tide would have to struggle to obtain.
    The soul clung to the stake, but his fear was wasted
    On an idealism he portrayed as being true.

The Harvester

As the river rose and climbed over the rocks,
    Each drop crept toward me.
    I bent down and submerged my arm.
    The dense blood cleansed my bones of all flesh.
    The current moaned, becoming greedy in its intention.
    The tide continued to rise as I extracted my arm.

With my intact hand, I calmed the troubled river
    By hovering my fingers above the crests of its waves.
    Slowly, the current became passive.
    The river knew I would tend to its every need.

I immediately halted the ritual burning of any flesh.
    Although, I would miss the aroma,
    I ordered certain laborers to collect all flesh
    And deliver it to the shoreline via meat wagons.
    The wheels would transport the deliveries of flesh
    To where the cliff's edge met with the river.
    The tumbling of the corpses against the rocky cliff
    And the splashing as they collided with the river
    Was a rhythmic pattern so tranquil and surreal.

The amount of haze omitted by the river
    Masked the true vastness of its size.
    A complete beast of nature,
    Carved from the anger of God himself
    And filled with the blood of his creations.

Pain pushes the shifts in tides.
    Hatred slashes the rocks with waves.
    To all the souls, it was a terrible relic,
    To me, it was a wonderful addition to my realm.

One flaw, if ever the river had one,
    Would be its inability to consume bone.
    The hardened material beset the river bed

Jones

And covered the shorelines with a pearl white hue.
The vision reminded me of broken sticks.
When the tides were at its lowest,
The bones revealed themselves.

To make it so only flesh would enter the river,
I burdened a condemned soul
With the task of removing the bones from the dead,
Prior to being loaded into the meat wagons.
The bones upon the riverbed were never added to.

A society was beginning to develop;
A civilization within the underworld,
Far from the land of God and the warmth of the sun.
A rocky canvas became our sky;
Trenches of dirt became our fields;
The stench of death became our wind.

Without having ever been to my realm,
The sinners were able to find their way.
Their eyes were lost, their thoughts emptied.
True nomads in every aspect.
All arriving to hear their fates;
To be held accountable for their sins.

My curiosity desired the knowledge
Of how each soul displeased God.
To learn how I had infected their hearts
Without ever actually meeting them.
To know which stories tempted them
From the path of the righteous.

Their bodies remained intact;
Their souls encased, ready for the reaping.
Once within my outer field,
The condemned souls roamed pointlessly

The Harvester

While their mind struggled to comprehend.
There was no clear path;
No precise method to the madness.
A path through my realm was needed
In order to funnel the souls to where I wanted them.
First, a separation process was needed.
The rotting flesh proved to be a mess
If the soul was imprisoned as they had arrived.
The soul was the true relic of man, the body was not.

A group was created in order to reap the humans
Of all flesh and bone prior to entering the city.
Named the Reapers; the chosen ones.
Four souls, all guilty of spreading my name,
Were burdened with robbing the dead of their flesh.

A small adjacent cave was excavated.
One of the most brutal areas,
The sounds of the slaughter
Could be heard from all corridors of the city.

The four Reapers were allowed individual thought.
A level of hatred for the humans
Had to reside within each of their minds
As the task required a certain level of disgust.
To mutilate another had to be based on emotions
So disfigured that neither pity nor remorse existed.

To do so, I fed their minds for days with memories
Of how they were bred into evilness
Toward a society that punished them.

Carrying elongated scythes and covered in black,
The hatred boiling within their veins
Revealed itself in unspeakable demeanors.
Their task altered their persona;

Jones

The blackness dwelling in their hearts came forth
And took hold of their characteristics.
An intimidation corrupted their mannerisms;
An intense power overcame their appearance.
Standing tall in posture, the four reapers
Struck fear in all that stood before them.

All flesh bearing souls left their bodies as trophies.
To not fracture the human mind, the cave was darkened.
The bodies were cast aside while the soul quickly exited
In order to not view its own cadaver.

To my dismay, the dead kept arriving.
To not overpopulate my city,
I would often times order the closing of the gates.
If they only knew what awaited them,
The dead would not be so anxious for entry.

I would summon the river and allow for a feast.
Standing upon the south wall, just above the gates,
I would watch as the swells tried to breach the cliffs.
The troubled river looked for my acceptance,
I made it clear that it would not topple my walls,
But to focus its efforts on the outlying fields.

The waves mutilated the flesh;
The tides swallowed the souls.
The stone walls fought against the river,
Holding back its onslaught.
The current left no portion of the fields untouched.
The flesh was chewed by the crests.
The tides gorged themselves and slowed the currents.
As the tide receded back into its trench,
The fields were littered with hills of bones.
I left the uneven terrain alone as I believed
It would slow the progress of new souls arriving.

The Harvester

Yet more leaked into my realm at an annoying pace.
I was unprepared for the aftermath of souls.
In the beginning, I thought I was only dealing with sin.
Spreading it like a disease.
But I was realizing there was so much more to my task.

I required more filtration areas to delay the incoming souls,
    I charged my servants to erect more gates,
    Allowing only small groups of souls
    To enter into the outer bone fields.

The once easy path to Hell
    Became contorted at the banks of the river,
    Where I could flood the fields if needed.
    However, the mindless souls began walking into the current,
    Much to the acceptance of the river.

Another wall and gate were constructed
    To push the awaiting souls back further
    From the shoreline, but I still required
    A way for the souls to travel through the river
    With a small degree of safety so that
    The majority would arrive to the awaiting Reapers.

As I pondered my options, Lucifer appeared beside me,
    Caressing his beard with one hand.
    He was appreciative of the pride I had
    And the accomplishments I introduced.

However, my mind was plagued with thoughts
    Both useless and unreasonable.
    I did not want his praise;
    I wanted his answer to my problem.
    He was incapable of providing my disease with a cure.

Jones

Frustration conjured within my blood.
>My eyes coated with red,
>I released my anger upon a large boulder,
>Tossing it violently into the river.
>Instead of sinking, the rock skipped atop the ripples.

The action gave me an idea.
>Two wooden docks, one on either side of the river,
>Were constructed, but were toppled by the current.
>Not wanting any such material penetrating its core,
>The river destroyed any attempt that was built.

My second attempt was successful.
>The new docks, forged from bone,
>Withstood the devastation of the currents..

A large ferry was built from bones
>And pushed through the rocky shoreline
>To where it met with its new possessor: the river.
>The waves crashed against the bone,
>Violently rocking the boat.
>The river comforted itself again
>As I stepped foot into the belly of the ferry.
>Acceptance was what I needed from the river;
>Trust was what I demanded.
>The current showed its understanding
>By remaining tranquil and serene.

The wide vessel was capable of carrying
>Hundreds of the dead at once across the river.
>And a laborer soul was needed for that task.

Weakened souls were easily discarded
>And never chosen for production tasks.
>Only the strong willed were selected,
>But they were difficult to find.

The Harvester

To the outer edges of my realm, I went.
I sought out strength and power.
An almost unattainable task within a sea of blabbering dead.
The closeness of the dead disgusted me.
Every touch and pull at my cloak sent me closer to wrath.

With a simple sway of my arms, a radius was gifted to me.
They were mindless, but not brazen enough to try again.
I grew my haven circle larger in the hopes
Of enticing just one to cross its threshold.
I waited patiently as I gazed around the crowd.
Within that dead cavern, who would be up for my task?

I desired a soul strong as their task would not be easy.
One with no fear as to why they ventured to my realm.
Someone distraught within the living and resentful.

I saw him towering above the rest.
A cloaked soul moving forward without care.
A man with no fear, pushing aside others.
His next step would separate himself from the rest.
With his next step, he would seal his fate.
With no weakness apparent,
He isolated himself from the others and neared me.

His height was twice mine;
His strength, more than all others combined.
I stopped him by placing of my hand on his chest.
His breathing was that of an ox bred for labor.
With a lack of scars, I could tell he was newly deceased.
His mind was tormented by visions of death,
But with no fear.

By merely being near him, I was able to see into his soul.
The ability to do so was new, but as I looked deeper
I could see who he was when he'd been alive.
He was a blacksmith that fell to the sin of wrath.

Jones

He became enraged when his mate was attacked
By a group of villagers and left for dead.
Distraught and unwilling to live after finding her,
He took his own life to be with his love.
A blade to his heart brought him to me.
As his beloved surely ascended to be with God,
He descended to me, and I was grateful.

All crimes of sin were meant to be here.
His sadness for his love still remained deep in his soul,
Untouchable by even myself.
The blade still resided within his beating, bruised heart.
I eased his distressed mind by looking into his eyes.
Through the winds of the cavern,
All felt his agony; all felt his pain.

He accompanied me to the land of the living,
Where we ventured back to his homeland.
His lack of knowledge of the attackers plagued him,
As they were far gone upon the discovery of his mate.
However, *I* was aware of them.
Working in the cornfields,
The four men kept their dark secret to themselves.
I imagined the blacksmith would want to meet them,
So we visited them while they worked.

The stalks of corn were swaying in the warm breeze.
The sun was bright and danced within the blue sky.
Whether my intentions were known or not,
The perfect weather slowly became hazy,
As if death itself was cradling the atmosphere.
The wind increased with a chill;
The sun hid behind the clouds.

God knew why I was there; he showed displeasure
With the changes in weather, but they were subtle,
And I perceived that as acceptance.

The Harvester

We stood on the edge of the field,
    Watching the four men busily collecting the crops.
    Having never seen them before,
    I had to connect the pieces for the blacksmith.
    A tear rolled down his face upon hearing my words.
    Since he never knew exactly what happened,
    I offered him the true vision of the event
    And he accepted by closing his eyes.

The four men followed his love from the village market
    While he was away collecting water.
    They overtook her with a brutality
    Of which she could not defend herself.
    Left to die under God's will, the men rummaged
    For artifacts not equaling the worth of a life.
    Choking on blood, she hoped for salvation.

Grief filled the wound of the blacksmith;
    Sorrow moistened his tongue.
    Disappointment for not being there
    To protect her watered his eyes.

No other words needed to be spoken.
    No other visions needed to be seen.
    I simply offered the blacksmith my scythe.
    A handle built from my sacrifice;
    A blade forged from my retribution.
    His reflection glistened off the metal with sorrow.
    His grip tightened as he looked to the field,
    Glaring at each one who had stolen his peace.

I did not witness his anger nor his rage,
    But I did hear the sounds of death spilling.
    My scythe could be seen breaching the yellow sea,
    Followed closely by arcs of blood raining down.
    The hollowed screams chased off lingering birds.

Jones

The sound of my scythe slicing through human bone
    Allowed me to follow his progress.
    As quickly as he had entered, he emerged in front of me
    With all four corpses, two on each shoulder,
    And a sense of pride within his eyes.
    No hesitation, no remorse.

He knelt before me, bowed his head
    And raised my scythe in appreciation.
    A justified revenge;
    An action granted to only those most deserving.

We returned back to the cavern in my realm.
    I allowed for the blacksmith to extract their souls.
    The disgust he showed was honorable to behold.
    No blade was used for extraction, only his bare hands
    Tore through the flesh of the four murderers.
    Each soul watched their body thrown so far
    That they were lost in the haze above the river.

To be constantly reminded of his loss
    And the torture his heart had endured,
    He swallowed the four souls deep within his chest
    Where they would serve him for eternity.

With his revenge subdued, his new task was to begin.
    I soothed the river slightly, by submerging one foot
    As I instructed the blacksmith to enter.
    My notion was to reduce the anger of the tides,
    Allowing him to feel the suffering of those entrapped.
    The waves tore at his flesh as he tried to stay afoot.
    The current then turned its attention to him,
    Swirled around, and swallowed him whole.

My realm had seen violence and brutality prior,
    But the unstableness of the river trembled the cavern.

The Harvester

Fleshless and angered,
The blacksmith rose from the boiling river.
His once blackened cloak was stained red.
The river spared no meat from his bones,
But left all internal organs untouched.
His ribcage expanded with every breath he took;
His bones crackled with every shift in movement.
His heart, still staked by the blade, pumped by the river;
His mind full of remembrance and understanding.

The ferry floated from the red haze of the cavern,
The bow split the bones as it reached the shoreline.
I gifted him a scythe with an elongated handle,
Long enough to reach down into the river bed.
The wooden shaft stained with the blood of his victims
And the battered dress of his mate
Tied to the top for all to see.

Before his destiny was to begin,
Another cleansing of the fields was in order.
With scythe in hand he walked back where dead waited.
The river needed to be fed
And who better to handle the task.

The power he displayed was perfection in my eyes.
With every swing of his weapon,
Flesh and blood flew amongst the dust filled air.
As the souls emerged, their bodies fell.
To cleanse his field, he sank his blade
Deep into the corpse piles and lifted a large amount.
What he did next appeased even my stubborn side
And insured that he was indeed the one for the task.
With a heavy rotation, he spun the shaft of his scythe
And tossed the lifeless bodies over the gate
Where they were greeted by the awaiting swells.

Jones

If angered for any reason,
    The wrath of the blacksmith would reveal itself.
    He would not have to answer to me regarding
    How often or how much he fed his river,
    But starvation was never an option.
    A dissatisfied river affected the entire realm.
    A satisfied river set the realm at ease.

⋗⋘⋗

Without even venturing to God's land and unleashing sin myself,
    My realm was being bombarded by more condemned souls.
    Cells were carved into every wall within the caverns,
    But still I required more.
    Additional massive caverns were hollowed out.

No traveling soul could avoid walking past the prisons.
    No traveling soul could avoid hearing
    The consecrated sounds of the sentenced.

Every wall, every corner
    Was speckled with the rusty bars of confinement.
    Suffering echoed through the connected caverns
    Like a song traveling between ears.
    There was no avoidance; there was only acceptance
    As to what would greet a soul upon arriving at Hell.

I reserved the largest cavern for judgment.
    Being the slowest of the filtration paths,
    Judgment required a field to hold the waiting souls.
    Each soul would be judged independently of others
    On their sins while in their living human state.
    Lesser sins would receive a sentence of citizen labor.
    Those deemed unfit for society,
    Would receive a sentence of isolation
    And a personal pit of despair

Filled with visions of madness and contempt.
The fate of punishment was not highly desirable
As each soul would became a part of the walls.
Once imprisoned, their mindless thoughts
Would be tormented to the edge of insanity.
The patterns could be intensified
If their mind could withstand the bombardment.

Upon the separation between soul and body,
The mind remained in control, but without thought.
The sheer terror the soul endured
During that process was beyond explanation.
The mortal mind is a wonderful relic;
Capable of individual thought and judgment.
Capable of unique personality traits.
The darkened side of a mind is equally as wonderful
With the ability to be inflicted with pain and suffering.

Sentences and judgments penetrate
The rational portion and disease it from within.
What is left is a controlled mind infected
With a personal destiny or fate upon my choosing.
As the souls rot in their cells,
Their minds are portraying my thoughts;
My desires for how I want their punishments.
My pain and suffering seals their dreams.
My sorrow clouds their visions.
For eternity, they are a part of me.

I believed God's plan was to change
The concept of mortal lives;
To be a dispute of one's will.
Prior, life was a celebration of faith,
An opportunity of peace, love and tranquility.
Living was a gift from God,

Jones

With everyday a serene appreciation
For what he had given the land.
Along the journey, the faith of God was challenged.
To what extent, I cannot speak of.

The human life altered itself and was pushed further away
From its creator so that a journey could be crafted.
Much like the filtration area of my realm,
God too had formed crossroads,
Slowing the travels and testing the minds of his following.
The glory of God was now hidden from the humans.
The once beautiful fields of ripened fruit
Were concealed from the mortal eyes.
The once tranquil horizons of mountains and valleys
Were buried far beyond the edge of the earth.

A separation between God and humans occurred quickly.
Most were devastated and saw the act as a betrayal.
Those who did, became roaming souls within my realm.
God himself delivered them to me.

Something challenged the faith of God;
Something displeased him greatly.
The once superior civilization of humans,
So perfect in every aspect,
So detailed in their orientations,
Was reduced to an unappreciative state.

The human defiance gave birth to my burden.
I myself am no more than a small twist
Within God's plan for the humans.
I serve only as an obstacle along his path.
I serve only to halt the progress.
My realm serves as an end path away from glory.

The Harvester

My palace was my acknowledgment.
    My courtyard was my celebration.
    My filtration was my enjoyment.
    My collection of souls was my crown.

My palace overlooked all from its hilltop position.
    Each sin added to the production of the city
    And became the life source of the realm.
    A flaw in one became a flaw in the overall system.

The city became my new farmland;
    The essence for my sanity and stability.
    I allowed nothing within my walls
    That provided me with displeasure.

My palace became my only true ally
    Within a place filled with deception and defiance.
    The walls offered me silence;
    The corridors offered me solitude.
    The inlets allowed vision of all areas within my realm,
    A vast empire of death and dismay,
    Of which I thanked God for.

IV: Encouragement

With my realm capable of running itself,
I was allowed the freedom
To further test the capabilities of society.
I ventured back to the land of the sun,
Observing the emotions of civilization.
No longer did society dwell within God's hands.

He unleashed the human mind
Like a captured beast desiring freedom from its chains.
The beast would either prosper under its own will,
Or fail miserably through its lack of guidance.
I am tasked to offer the humans the guidance
No longer granted by their creator.

From city to city, I traveled.
Whispers of my existence
Scoured the land well before my arrival.
Word spread of my existence
Through every passing caravan,
Through every roaming nomad,
Through every falling leaf.
However, proof was buried within my realm.
Only God knew of my true reality.

The Harvester

I was rumored and distorted within the tales.
    I had been called a diseased, plague ridden horse
    That trampled upon the weak.
    I had been described as a horrific wind gust,
    Which left only bones in its path.

After God punished my theft through the sacrifice of goats,
    I secretly spared two in a far reached cave
    To restore the species and reserve their existence.
    Not only did I use the humans as my minions,
    But I also sent the goats to every farmland, every town.

The human mind was eloquent in design.
    The hearing of merely one word could trigger emotion.
    As the mind struggled to translate what was heard,
    The thought process paused to collect the information.

My name heard through the ears of the faithful
    Proved to be devastating,
    Eliciting a reaction of fear or anger.
    Seldom did complete denial occur.
    God foresaw the outcome prior to my sentence of sin.
    He observed the downfall of human faith
    Far before it had begun.
    As a sign of disparagement,
    He offered his beloved humans a test.
    Those who passed remained with him;
    Those who failed became a part of me.

With the crossroads well established,
    And the awards and punishments for each apparent,
    I journeyed across the lands with my temptations
    With only one goal in mind;
    To infect every human that crossed my path.

Jones

I left no hope or faith when I departed a village.
　　What I delivered was a choice to society;
　　Tempting them to either side was not difficult.
　　Some were already searching for me before I arrived.

Society remained strong and created faithful groups
　　In hopes to increase their availability to the heavens.
　　And thus society gave birth to religion.
　　An act of defiance to my cause, but to my acceptance,
　　As it gave me plenty of opportunity to inflict sin.
　　Religion would be battered like the shattered faith.

My first encounter with religion was amongst
　　A group of farmers on the edge of a modest town.
　　Mistaking me for a mere nomad, they accepted me.
　　Their words were that of praise,
　　But their actions told a different story.

The leader wore a delicate white robe
　　And preached the word of God.
　　I saw opportunity within him, as the word of God
　　Was not for any ground walking human to hear.
　　For a human to personify God to their level,
　　Was as much of a sin as the murderous act of wrath.
　　I pondered his reaction to my realm
　　As I was assured that I would see him there.

Still he preached to all who would offer their ear.
　　He spoke of another religious group.
　　I saw hesitation in his word choice;
　　I saw a redness glow against his skin.
　　Religion was a beautiful notion,
　　As long as one believes
　　What others intend for them to believe.

The Harvester

An opportunity presented itself to me.
    One that to this day conjures itself
    Within all forms of religion.
    An opportunity to show the sheer vastness
    And contamination of the mortal mind.

Faith was gifted by God in the beginning.
    Faith was then challenged by God.
    Faith was then destroyed by the humans.

He preached how the others were wrong in their idealism,
    How their lessons had forsaken them
    And changed the one true path to glory.

I could not conceal a grin any longer.
    It was the essence of my task,
    Spewing from the mouth of a preacher.
    Judging others based on their interpretation.
    Society would never be the same again.
    That small inclination of hatred toward others
    Would prove to be my largest companion.
    Every opportunity; every crevice of doubt
    Would be an advantage to my cause.

The preacher within that wooden shack,
    Spreading religion, would serve as my first temptation.
    With Lucifer studying the other group
    And whispering sinful notions
    Toward the farmers and how they worshipped,
    The stones were beginning to shift.
    What would a human do, in the name of God?
    How far would they drift in their belief system?
    And still the preacher preached on,
    With words of purification and acceptance,
    Of which he practiced neither.

Jones

I became fascinated by the preacher,
    As everyone believed his words.
    There was much to admire about him,
    His stature and ability to control an audience.
    I was curious to how far off the path he would venture.
    There was instability with manmade religion.
    I needed more clarification as my ambition was lofty.

The city became the dwelling for Lucifer and myself
    As we observed the new religious aspirations of man.
    The concept was clear;
    Associating one's self with others with the same idealism.

Confusion arose about what was being taught.
    Lucifer and I often pondered the realism
    Of the teachings and the basis for the subjects.
    It was quite astonishing how meritless words
    Presented in a well atoned speech
    Could distort the very foundation of individual faith.

The sermons continued with every setting of the sun.
    The tone of the preacher when speaking of others
    Became blistered with hidden meanings.

Boredom crept to me like a snow drift
    As I sat in the back of the congregation.
    My task would be much easier
    If I was allowed to unleash death upon all,
    But alas that was not my choice.

Through the mindless dribble of words, I heard it.
    Through the sea of confusion, I heard it.
    An idealism leaking through the teeth of the preacher,
    So distraught, so horrific that even I was ashamed.
    His chosen words shattered the notion of peace
    Amongst the common human race regardless.

The Harvester

He spoke of his God as a separate entity
From those who practiced differently.

The thought fed into the minds of all who heard the speech.
    A separation occurred that night, one that would plague
    The human civilization upon my alteration.

The limits of the separation were tested.
    Two unique groups believing in one entity,
    So demented that God would then become two entities.
    Humans never ceased to astound me;
    So much potential with sin.
    The preacher continued with imprecise words of my life.
    He began by forming my name over his tongue.
    He spoke of me as a serpent,
    Slithering through the long grass hunting for prey.

He spoke of my characteristics with features of a goat;
    Horns atop my head, an elongated beard upon my chin.
    He continued by depicting reddish, hardened skin.

A fallen angel, a demonic soul sent to punish the humans.
    His depiction of my tale, my journey, was greeted
    With much anticipation by all who heard his words.

Much like the misunderstanding of God,
    I too was a fish in the sea of confusion.
    I suppose I could have torn the spine from the preacher
    So that everyone would know
    The true meaning of my name.

With Lucifer observing the other group,
    We were able to share similarities as well as differences
    That could be exploited to augment the situation.

Jones

We summoned Mammon for greed and Levi for envy.
    The combination would build hatred from within.
    Greed would be adapted to the religion
    In the forms of monetary demands and power.
    Envy with regards to the size of the congregations.
    A compounding effect built from sin
    And led along by demons.

Each sun brought about new injections of sin.
    Each moon brought about new visions of resentment
    So detailed that each of the preachers spoke of them
    And claimed them as words gifted from Heaven.
    The preachers swore the visions were real
    And that it was God whose words flowed through them.
    But it was not God's words of which he spoke;
    They were mine.
    The goal was simple;
    To push the boundaries of human religion.

Hatred was nurtured which led to arguments.
    Tempers were reaching an apex.
    Arguing in the name of God was a despicable trait,
    But I saw something more disastrous
    In the form of a clinched fist.
    Would the humans be so blinded,
    That they would dare commit bloodshed?

I visited a preacher of my group to understand his reasoning.
    I sat alongside him as he slept.
    His troubled mind danced through visions of faith.
    I eased his dreams so that my words would be heard.
    He despised the other preacher for one reason,
    That he did not share the same beliefs.

There was a natural corruption established
    Within every mortal mind;

The Harvester

Well hidden beneath the traits necessary
To intertwine oneself within a society.
Without temptation, all would remain well.
All would see that of which they seek.
Ignorance when approached by temptation
Was a desired trait sought after,
But blinded within the eyes of man.

The preachers tempted their audience with words;
Whereas the audience desired the knowledge for faith.
A perfect relationship forged by a false prophet.

Seeking refuge from the congregation outside,
I found myself on the banks of a flowing river.
The sounds of the water desperately trying to overtake
The large boulders reminded me of my farmland
And the river I used to cleanse my tools.
I often travel back to my farm, if only in my mind.
I question its existence as a physical place.
I can imagine every aspect of the farm
From the height of the wheat
To the rolling hills of the surrounding lands.

I understood that the farm served as my staging ground,
To wait for God's calling, but was the farm?
Was it another predetermined thought pattern
Much like the seven sins?

What is real may not be what is perceived by the mind.
I believed that I was living *through* sin.
I believed I was a carpenter, a blacksmith,
A tailor, but the reality was that I was none of them.
I did not try to contemplate the powers of God
Nor his ability when ruling over the land,
But my mind was plagued with questions,
Of which I would never find the answers.

Jones

If only I could find my farmland;
    Seeing it would have relieved my confusion.
    I was forced to wonder
    If I had a real life prior to isolation in the cave.
    Was the farm, goats, cottage
    All a part of my manufactured destiny?

The river was soothing to watch.
    The unpredictable nature of the water captured my soul
    And eased the questions from my mind.

For a brief moment, I was not who I was.
    For a brief moment, sin did not exist.
    For a brief moment, I was not a servant.

I was merely a farmer tending to his livestock,
    Observing a storm rolling over the valley.
    The clash of the darkened, blue sky
    Against the swaying green grass was mesmerizing.
    The cool, crisp breeze carried an aroma of wheat
    And forced the blades of grass to dance.

The storm crept over the mountain range
    Like a mother blanketing a child.
    The blackened clouds suffocated the crops.
    The scent of depression stole the aroma.
    I imagined God pushing the storm forward.
    The sun no longer provided warmth and stability.
    In its place were tormented, swirling clouds
    Pulling weak rooted vegetation from the ground.

My eyes swelled with fear as a funneling cloud
    Ripped through my wheat field destroying every stalk,
    Carving the land until every seed was tossed aside.

The Harvester

Lightning danced across the sky
    Providing brief moments of light.
    Through my shielded eyes I saw the cloud-beast,
    Spiraling and fervent by untouched land.

I could do nothing but mourn the devastation of the vision.
    The act of remembering served as my downfall.
    I had ventured to the farm too many times.
    A distraction along my own path of God,
    A questioning of faith.

I became resentful of God by envisioning my farm.
    I became disrespectful of God by questioning realism.
    For that I was punished.
    My eyes bore witness to the destruction
    Of everything that I held dear.

The sky rotated with vengeance,
    And the ground trembled beneath me.
    My cottage shook uncontrollably
    As the walls splintered and became unfastened.
    The very foundation of the cottage buckled.

I sat alone in a valley of dirt.
    Everything was gone.
    My only soothing vision; all gone.
    I felt my soul deteriorating.
    I struggled to stay afloat even as the sun peaked.

God had given me an answer.
    He had taken everything.
    My eyes swelled with tears.

Without a place to visit, without a thought to conceive,
    I would never envision my farmland again.
    The vision faded against the current of the river.

Jones

Through my eyes,
    I have seen faith of one become that of many.
    Through my ears,
    I have heard God's tale twisted and confused.
    All believed by those who practiced the same.
    I have observed good souls bend their chosen fates
    By merely stopping and listening.
    Curiosity, although not a sin,
    Would serve as the greatest temptation.
    I too was curious about the element of anger
    And its influence upon religion and actions.
    The clinched fist, a single gesture of defiance.

Could religion be tainted to the edge of misconception,
    Where two visions become so varied in description
    That those who follow, view difference as a threat?

Each night we visited the preachers;
    Each morning they spoke our words,
    Translating every single one as that of their God.
    The message of each was the same;
    Hear me speak the word of God,
    Entrust your faith to me.
    Perception devastated the groups
    As different ideologies prospered.
    Gestures of envy and greed filled conversations.
    Feelings of glorified hierarchy flowed freely
    Through judging eyes,
    Forging relationships plagued by bitterness.

Disassociation formed between the groups.
    I was intrigued by the implementation.
    The mindless congregations believed and followed
    Every word the preachers spoke in their sermons.

The Harvester

Mayhem would serve as the course during a festival.
    Both groups were amongst the crowd.
    The whispers tormenting their thoughts and beliefs.
    Empowered by the preacher and embellished,
    The words spoke of strategic tactics of power.
    A merciless vision of civil recourse and determination
    Embodied the essence of each preacher and his pawns.
    Within that festival, within that celebration,
    Blood was boiling, tempers were breaking.

Along with my demons, I waited.
    The large fire resided within the center of the courtyard.
    The vastness of the blaze fought back the frigid weather
    And illuminated every face that looked upon it.
    The fire danced effortlessly.

A spark was what I needed,
    A subconscious act of turmoil
    So precise that would escalate into confrontation.
    I tasked Beelzebub to conjure a plan.
    A plan devious enough to finally revolt the preachers.

Beelzebub, deviating from my initial idea,
    Picked up an apple and tossed the fruit through the fire.
    The red skin caught ablaze and guided a trail of smoke.
    The apple struck the preacher directly in his head,
    Sending rinds scattering amongst the crowd.
    I looked to Beelzebub,
    Who was grinning from ear to ear.

After removing remnants of the fruit from his hair,
    The preacher turned red,
    Not from the apple, not from the fire,
    But from anger.

Jones

For the purpose of seeing the glorious opportunities
And the sought after sentence of labor.
Confinement could send a soul into a chaotic state.
An essence of the mortal mind remained
With the soul upon the separation from body.
The brittle state would be stricken with reality
As the slow duration of their stay
Took ahold of their thought patterns
And decided which visions were seen.

If ever a soul was deemed unfit for confinement,
They were considered a failure.
A personal cell overlooking the city
Was an endowment that would never be insulted.
Depending upon the state of the mind,
Whether correctable or lost,
The soul would either be granted a new sentence
Or pushed through their opened cell door
And allowed to plunge into the hungry river.

While I was away, the howls of the imprisoned
Echoed through the cavern in a low growl.
Upon my return, silence reigned.
I did not foresee my sheer hatred for souls.
I did not imagine having to overlook them.
My task was to unleash sin, but that had altered.
I tolerated what was asked of me,
But I did not have to befriend those that I encountered.

My anger with my own sentence was well known.
To release my pure despise for the human race,
I often visited the outer tunnels
To where the dead corpses plummeted from the sky;
Sent by the angels of God to begin their afterlife.
The angels had no remorse
When tossing them into my fields
And I would show even less upon my welcoming.

The Harvester

No nightmare would ever equal the sight for mortal eyes
    Than arriving within a mysterious land of death
    And coming face to face with me, its creator.

Each soul infested body, randomly chosen.
    I did not know which was worse,
    Being a soul selected for annihilation,
    Or being a soul witnessing the destruction of another.
    To have that vision embedded in one's mind
    As they began their path of darkness was brutal.

My purpose within the outer caves
    Was to merely release wrath
    In order to soothe my angered intentions.
    My scythe carving through fresh human bodies
    Granted me that release.

I would choose a field and wait within the darkness.
    They would fall into my darkened pit;
    The collision against the solid ground
    Was no match for the mortal body.
    The mind was stricken of sight and sound.

Moans of agony always began the awakening process.
    I allowed the mind to struggle
    With the acceptance that its body was wrongfully led
    To a place of unknown origin.
    The mind instructs its follower to rise
    In order to study the environment.
    As the eyes roamed for any sort of light,
    They would receive only the glistening of my blade.
    Their hands outreached to grasp anything for support
    Both physically and mentally.
    Fear of the dark alone was enough to cripple a mind.

Jones

To not allow wrath to control my complete emotions,
    I often stepped forward to gift my visitor a personable
    Object to relate to within the dark.
    Calmness of the mind relaxed the torturous unknown.
    The hands studied my face.

I did not need to offer that peace, but I did for the idea
    That I wished I had been gifted the same in return.
    Upon the sigh of relief,
    A gasp of tranquility from the mouth of the stranger,
    I would always be reminded of the hardships
    I faced in the seven day stint in my prison.
    The sorrow of the unknowing between life and death.
    The very hardship I would deliver to those chosen
    To find themselves within my fields.

My blade made the extraction from deep within their chest.
    My grip around their soul proved my power.
    The soul was burdened with the unavoidable task
    To watch the sheer destruction of its body.

Already confused by observing their corpse,
    The soul would try desperately to re-enter its shell.
    The thought was prevalent, but useless.
    The soul could not turn away as its body
    Was disfigured beyond recognition.
    The soul was then allowed to continue towards the city.
    I dared not think about my wrath left uncontrolled.
    My release was justified
    And meant to appease the stability of the realm.
    My own personal imprisonment
    Within caverns full of the dead
    Even tested my sanity,
    As I struggled with my own reality.
    I despise the humans as they are granted choices.
    They are allowed to succeed.

The Harvester

I am envious of man; I am envious of choice.
In return, I offer no pity on them.
I offer no remorse to those I torment.

Your faith does not matter to me.
Your level of belief in God does not matter to me.
Your level of sin matters to me.

V: Lamb

My name has become well versed across the land.
It flows through the ears of the weak
And battles with the strong.
It passes over the lips of the great
And lifts with the tongues of the dead.
It has become a symbol of fear.

I have shed many emotions.
I have been confused by my memories;
Angered by my visions.
I have been resentful of the humans;
Tempted by my own sins.
I have been guilty of greed, lust, envy,
Pride, sloth, gluttony and wrath.
I have been hurt from the pain; afraid from the fear.
I have been depressed by my mind;
Weakened at my crossroads.
But there was one emotion that I had not yet endured.
There was one emotion that was hidden from me
Throughout all I had experienced.

An emotion which would be my undoing.
An emotion directed toward God himself.

The Harvester

One so detrimental that it should be the eighth sin.
The emotion of disappointment.

God had forsaken me and cursed my faith with doubt.
All of which occurred with the birth of a son.

During one of my travels to ensure the progress of sin,
I had been visiting a local preacher
Who broke free from my scripted words
And spoke of a son; a Lamb of God.
From my slumbering state, I awoke with greedy ears.
It was infallible that God would have a son
And for what purpose; what cause?
I became angry with myself for falling victim
To the preacher's story of enlightenment.

Outside, I was met with joy and anticipation;
Both of which I despised greatly.
With my sins fully entrenched within society,
It should not be fathomable to have such pleasure.
With the threat of my realm being their eternity,,
It was impossible to show such happiness.

The words of the preacher echoed through walls.
He said that God would soon visit a virgin
With the task of giving birth to a son.

I made my way to a different city.
While walking the corridors, I heard the tale once more.
A prophet standing on the corner spewing of the child.
All ears that heard him believed his words.
They left his presence with smiles.
An aura of happiness was shielding them from my sins.

Such a tale of deception that challenged my own.
Had one of my demons conjured that demented tale?

Jones

Every story had a beginning,
Even the twisted ones.

To study the foundation of the tale,
    I chose to follow a preacher not yet infected.
    For days, I appeared as his shadow.
    The answer in which I sought
    Did not arrive as easily as I had imagined.
    To live the life of a preacher bored me,
    But one night while the preacher slept,
    A cool breeze flowed into his abode.
    Hidden well within the shadows,
    I watched as an angel flew into his room.
    She hovered over him and whispered into his ear.
    The servants of God visiting preachers?
    My mind plagued me with questions.
    I remained in the shadows until the angel left.
    Upon the rise of the sun,
    I followed the preacher to his congregation.
    As his gathering filtered in to their seats.
    His cheerfulness spread amongst the audience.
    A new religious notion counteracting my own.
    Why was the birth of a son important to mankind?

Every city I walked through, every village
    Spread the story of the upcoming child.
    Sins became overshadowed.
    My work, my deeds, my conquest;
    All pushed aside.

I prayed to God for understanding,
    But received nothing in return.
    I prayed to God for my course to remain true,
    But received nothing in return.

The Harvester

With no word or sign from God,
    My curiosity carved my insides
    As I spoke with locals from a village.
    They were loading up their horses with resources.
    I asked them where they were traveling to.
    They responded that they were traveling east
    To see the child and worship at his manger.
    My mind became disruptive
    As the birth of the son became true.
    I asked if I could travel with them
    As I too, wished to worship.

A desolate land full of sand was to be our goal.
    The dry air was to my liking, but the travelers' joy
    Was devastating upon my blackened heart.
    The clear, darkened skies provided our landscape
    With the brightest stars I had ever seen.

We crested a large sand dune
    And saw our destination within the horizon.
    A trail of nomads, gypsies, peasants and prophets
    Waited for their chance to worship the child.
    I felt more like a stranger than ever before,
    But I desired to know the origin.

As I neared, it became apparent that I was not welcomed.
    A small root exited the sand and took hold of my ankle.
    The sand beneath me began to sink quickly,
    But I grasped the reins of the horse to pull me out.

I noticed an old woman ahead of us.
    Her stride was not as strong as the others.
    I came upon her while she glared at me
    And began to sing the hymn I knew so well.
    It was the song of the banshee.

Jones

Her presence made me uneasy,
But I continued with my travels.

I had no intentions with the child
  Other than to see for myself if the story was true.
  So why the attention and obstacles?
  What was the child to become
  That protection was poured
  Down upon him from the skies?

The banshee remained close, matching my every footstep.
  I could see the top of the manger above the crowd.
  Another old hag appeared on the opposite side of me.
  The nomads knelt before the manger with gifts in hand,
  Neither of which I intended to do.
  However, to not anger my guides,
  I pulled a golden goblet from a satchel.

There was a peace in the air; a tranquility like no other.
  An alignment of the stars;
  A moon, the fullest I have ever laid eyes upon.
  More of the manger came into view.
  Kings and shepherds stood on either side.
  Various animals rested peacefully.

Before the manger, I stood.
  Before the shepherds, I stood.
  Before the kings, I stood.

Each of their eyes staring at me
  As if they knew who I was.
  My name had traveled far,
  But no face ever traveled with it.
  My demeanor was left untouched;
  Only the hags would have known me.

The Harvester

I held the goblet in my hand
    And took one step toward the child.
    The hands of the banshees grabbed my arms.
    The kings brandished their swords;
    The shepherds pointed their staves.
    I stood in silence, unsure as to what was occurring.
    I was not welcome there;
    My gift was deemed unworthy.

I looked to the swords pointing at me.
    Their gestures angered me, and I envisioned myself
    Using their very own weapons against them.
    However, being held by two banshees
    Altered my thoughts.
    The kings were not kings;
    The shepherds were not shepherds.
    All servants of God ordered to protect the child.
    Their souls told their stories;
    Their eyes portrayed their tasks.

The only one untouched
    Was the mother caressing the child.
    A true love from a true soul.
    Admirable to my mind.

The swords of the kings remained steady.
    The staves of the shepherds were held by strong hands.
    I was not positioned well to fall victim to my pride.

The child became unsettled by the length of my stay.
    The kings gestured to the hags who tried to pull me along,
    But I held my ground and did not move.
    I looked to the kings, then to the mother.
    Her eyes were kind.
    She was a blessing to behold as she did not know me,
    Therefore she could not judge.

Jones

In her mind, I was allowed to worship like the others.
In her thoughts, I was welcomed.
She thanked me for when no one else would.

As I bowed my head with respect, I backed away
    Causing my two guides to release their grips.
    The kings and shepherds hid their weapons
    As the next worshipper in line approached.

The hags followed closely behind me until I was far away.
    From the mountains of sand, I could see the manger
    And the waves of people awaiting to worship the child.
    The son of God was indeed born, but for what purpose?
    I stared at my goblet seeking answers.
    The unwanted trinket was left in the sand
    Along with my unanswered prayers.

I walked back to the line of worshippers,
    But not close enough to be noticed.
    I befriended another group of nomads from the far east
    On a quest to allow their eyes to gaze upon the baby.
    How important was the birth to mankind?

While I walked with them,
    A thin man in the caravan caught my eye.
    I brushed up against him, our shoulders meeting.
    My voice infected his ears, controlling his thoughts.
    I slid a dagger underneath his cloak
    Accompanied with my demands.
    He no longer traveled for worship;
    He no longer ventured for salvation.
    His path no longer led him toward God.
    I bid my farewells to the group and waited hilltop.

Group after group came and worshipped.
    The man soon found himself in front of the child.

The Harvester

The kings stared at the peasant before them.
His pressured emotions made themselves known.
His indications set the child's protectors on alert.
The grips of the kings met with their sword handles.
The shepherds clinched their staves.
I could tell he was afraid to complete the task.

I whispered into the air;
    As courage finally revealed itself within his eyes
    As his hand revealed the dagger,
    The guards converged upon him with great fury.
    He was dragged away from the manger.

As time went by, the word of the birth spread
    Across the land much quicker than I had imagined.
    His tale became twisted much like my own.
    We shared a common thread;
    We were both faithful to the same God.

Through the sermons, our names became distant.
    Through the religions, a separation had occurred.
    I had my followers; the Son had his.

As I tortured the weak, he held onto the strong.
    Those who were victims of my sins,
    Lessened in size within my realm
    Prompting me to travel in search of more answers.

I came upon a group of traveling gypsies.
    Their wagons could barely support the cargo.
    Their souls told the tales of sin.
    Each a sufferer from my temptations,
    But still they traveled in search of the Lamb.
    Surely they could not be helped or saved by the Son
    As they each belonged to me.

Jones

Curious to learn what they hoped to achieve,
    I asked about their intentions.
    They spoke of repenting for their sins;
    A cleansing of their souls
    That would allow them to enter God's kingdom.

I became offended by their words,
    But still allowed them to speak.
    They believed the Son could purify their souls
    If only they repented in front of him.
    A practice of remorse for actions; the opposite of pride.

I was not angry at the nomads, but I desired their deaths.
    The wheels of their wagons
    Would not reach the holy city that day . . . or ever.
    The sins of the damned would not be cleansed.
    Their souls would remain within my grasp.

I walked along the same road leading to the city
    And reaped any wandering traveler
    From whom the word 'repent' escaped their lips.
    The practice troubled me, making me unstable.
    It haunted my dreams and entangled my thoughts.
    Why would the Son cleanse the sins created
    By his own father and unleashed by a servant?

My task, my burden, was being denied
    And granted approval by God himself.
    I desired answers, so I continued to the city,
    Punishing those who traveled the same path
    To appease my own steady confusion.

The Son had become quite the minister
    With disciples and worshippers of his speech.
    I observed him from a distance
    As he was well protected within the city.

The Harvester

They portrayed themselves as prophets,
But they were no prophets.
Their eyes did not worship the stars.
Their eyes observed anyone who came near.
They were the inner circle of the minister.
To my eyes, their souls told a different tale.
One of justification and sanctuary
To ensure that the Son was guarded.

I sat upon a roof with my hooded cloak concealing my face.
My roaming eyes and eager ears were all I needed.

He was always well sheltered within his disciples,
So much so that no peasant could near him.
They walked with a great sense of power.
I would often test the limits
By consuming the minds of weakened peasants.
My words led them directly into the gatherings.
The Son's following allowed no one near.
Their strength was admirable and their resolve
Was swift and hidden from the eyes of others.
Their cloaks concealed their motions.
They encircled the Son at all times.
They walked when he walked, they fed when he fed.
They were an extension of him
Much like my demons were of me.

When the Son spoke, his disciples would kneel
Forming a tight circle of protection.
The outreached hands of the peasants
Were always graciously pushed aside,
But on occasion, one was allowed to near
And enter within the circle.
The Son's power of healing drew gasps from the crowd.

Jones

The eyes of the disciples
    Roamed the crowd in search of disturbances.
    It was clear the Son was a part of a plan.
    I was eager to understand how the two plans connected.

The next sun brought a gathering of peasants,
    Where the Son and his disciples
    Addressed the crowd of the worshippers.
    I edged closer to the outer banks to hear his words.
    The disciples all stood,
    Their eyes penetrating my skull with their stares.

I remained still, with hopes to not draw attention,
    But one of the disciples broke the circle.
    Through the crowd he walked,
    As I lowered my head, drifting back into the shadows.

Within the cascaded dark of wooden cargo crates,
    I waited as the disciple stood at the threshold of light.
    I required more knowledge regarding his master,
    And I was not prepared to battle a servant of God.
    That was not my intention.
    My voice shifted with the wind,
    Corrupting the mind of a random worshipper
    Who began a loud outburst toward the Son.
    The disturbance summoned the disciple back.

As the moon rose against the darkened sky,
    The Lamb preached on the outskirts of the city
    Far from the judging eyes of the local officials.
    Surrounded by his followers, the Son preached
    About repenting against the sins of the world.

I needed to understand his theory.
    I could not do so within my current state,
    My stench of death was too overbearing.

The Harvester

I grabbed the nearest peasant.
He became an extension of my soul
With his movements all my own.
His confused mind was filled with sinful memories.
His weakened body disgusted me,
But he would serve me well.

A line formed to allow for the repenting process to begin.
As I awaited my turn—inside the body of the peasant—
I noticed soldiers and city officials standing back.
My ears were filled with envy toward the Son regarding
His hierarchy and demeanor amongst the society.
There was a concern regarding his stature.
There was a threat of an uprising against the law.
It seemed I was not the only one with curiousity.

My tongue held back his voice,
My arms held back any movement,
As the disciples looked to him with heavy, judging eyes.
Allowed to near, he stood before the Son,
The closest I had ever been,
Even if it was not within my own body.

His soul was the purest I had seen.
His face provided serenity with eyes of kindness.
There was no question that he was the Son of God,
But I was not there to admire him;
I was there to gain an understanding.

The peasant kneeled down before him.
His white cloak resting upon the ground.
His hand laid upon the bowed head.
No words were said,
But I felt his eyes within the mind, searching for sins.
The soul of the peasant was caressed gently.
His soul was held by me,

Jones

But drifting toward the visions portrayed by the Son.
My hold was slipping; my grasp loosened.
Forced to exit the body, my eyes became that of my own.
My ears heard only the sounds around me.
I was no longer in control of the peasant's soul.
My temptations and embedded sins no longer existed
As he was cleansed of everything deemed unworthy.

I had seen the act of repenting
   And the gift of forgiveness first hand.
   A renewed soul stricken from my path,
   Allowed to travel upon the holy way.
   Every sinner, every soul that belonged to me
   Could be released from my chosen fate
   And granted a new beginning in the form of faith.

That was not welcomed within my thoughts.
   To steal all that I had acquired, all I had been through;
   My agony, my despair, my burden.

I looked upon the Lamb with resentment.
   His task was to undo all that I had accomplished.
   A new religion established to allow the humans
   A prosperous crossroad leading away from my realm.
   Why inflict sin, if it was to be removed?
   Why conjure evil, if good was to overcome?

On a warm day, I saw something I had not seen before;
   I saw the Son wandering alone away from the city.
   Curiosity plagued my mind as I followed him.
   Deep into the desert he traveled, carrying nothing.
   As the sun vanished and the brightest of stars appeared,
   He sat within the sand and stared at the sky.

The Harvester

I observed from a distance,
    The moon bathing him in an ominous way.
    Days passed and yet he remained in the desert
    Without food or water.
    He spoke no words and no one came to look for him;
    Completely alone with his thoughts,
    I decided to test his boundaries of faith.
    My whispers funneled through his ears as he slept,
    Then caressed his thoughts during the day.
    I spoke of the seven sins,
    But his mind battled every temptation that was offered.

His spirit was well intact, and he countered
    Every sin with its virtue.
    When tempted with wrath, he gave patience.
    When tempted with gluttony, he spoke of temperance.
    With greed, he offered charity.
    With sloth, he responded with diligence.
    Envy, he provided kindness
    And with pride, he acted with humility.

My frustration grew with every failed attempt.
    My anger raged.
    For forty days and forty nights,
    He remained in the desert.
    For forty days and forty nights,
    I was unable to break him.

Even as he became famished,
    His mind remained wholesome.
    He was everything I hated; a pure soul.
    On the last night, his disciples came
    And carried him back to the city.

With the stars as my witness
    And the moon as my judgment,

Jones

I vowed to disturb the undisturbed.
I vowed to disrupt the untouchable.

I started with the envious city officials,
    As a mortal was much more easier to corrupt.
    My whispers carried the visions of a revolution
    If the Son was allowed to continue his sermons.
    His ministry needed to halt for the sanctity of the city.

My seeds were embedded well in the minds of the officials.
    They pondered the Son during the days
    And watched him from the shadows at night.
    His arrest was approaching and necessary,
    But his congregation was always by his side.
    Civil unrest would be chaotic if the Son
    Was taken from them in front of their eyes.
    His followers would sacrifice all justification.
    A separation from his congregation was needed.

I surveyed them from afar for quite some time;
    Their mannerisms, their postures, their gestures toward
    The audience and toward one another.
    I needed that small hesitation;
    A small unlatched door to allow my entry.

They were perfect in all aspects which was frustrating,
    But one day within the marketplace,
    I saw an opening; a weakness in one of the disciples.

On many occasions, the circle would purchase food
    Without ever caring about the amount of coin given,
    But a certain disciple would always count
    To be sure that no excess was wasted.

A doubt in the righteousness of man.
    A greed in the fulfillment of coin.
    A smile upon my face.

The Harvester

His greed; his envy would be my tools.
    His mind would serve as my lumber.

The eyes of the disciple began to roam.
    The ears of the disciple listened more intently.
    The dreams of the disciple became unbalanced.

His body continued to protect the Son,
    But his mind ventured from the task.
    His physical actions resented his thoughts.
    An internal struggle against my will ensued.
    The body would not be victorious.

He became so entangled within my words
    That his greed of coin grew
    To thievery amongst the vendors,
    All hidden well from the eyes of his master.

I gathered a grouping of officials
    To work alongside the disciple.
    The officials needed the Son to be alone,
    The disciple needed to appease his greed.
    I needed for both to obtain what they desired.

There were no stars within the sky;
    There was no moon to provide light.
    I sat rooftop and watched as he met with the city officials
    Within a corridor hidden in the shadows of the city.

Over the next few days,
    He had influenced the other disciples
    With envy of the righteousness of their master.
    The Son had all to gain; the following had nothing.
    The disciple infected their ears that he would
    Better serve as ruler of the religious kingdom

Jones

And those who followed
Would receive riches beyond their dreams.

His words clashed with their faith,
But curiosity began to overwhelm their minds.
Their eyes saw what he had envisioned.
Their ears heard what he had portrayed.
Each began to view their master with resentment.
A slippery path of distrust and disobedience,
All buried behind their task of protection.
He offered the Son a prayer of solitude
With no congregation; no distractions.
The Son was grateful to his friend
And was left alone within the sanctuary of his abode.

Silence fell upon the city as he summoned the guards
And led them to the location of the praying Son.
As the door opened,
He acted like he was protecting his master,
But his conceived plan was nothing of the sort.

Arrested for treason against the city,
The Son was shackled and imprisoned.
There would be no more repenting.
My souls would belong to me;
My sins would remain unhealed.
There would be no more salvation.

As the Son was bound and staked;
Left to die under the hot sun;
I knelt beneath him as his blood dripped.

I unfolded my hood, revealing my face.
He did not look to me with anger.
He did not look to me with judging eyes.
He merely looked to me as a man.

The Harvester

Why was he not angered?
　　Why was God's vengeance not handed down?

I did not understand his resolve.
　　I did not understand why God would allow for this.
　　Searching the mind of the Son, I found the answer;
　　The one I had been in long search of.
　　The answer that would begin my fall from grace.
　　A vision I wished I had never seen;
　　One that would forever alter my path.

Deep in his mind I dwelled;
　　My soul entwined with his.
　　A sense of companionship;
　　A uniting of our symbolisms.

Visions of his birth as the savior.
　　His ministry, his sermons, his disciples;
　　All chosen by God himself.
　　His teachings to the peasants,
　　His healing of the wounded,
　　His practice of repenting
　　Were all visible within his mind.

He had foreseen all of his life before he was even born.
　　A purpose, a reasoning created by God.
　　He was gifted for the prosperity of mankind.
　　He had known my arrival at the manger,
　　My corruption in the city;
　　All foreseen by his young eyes.
　　He had predicted his arrest.
　　All allowed to occur
　　Under the guidance of the master plan.

He was born to die, but for what cause?
　　Why had our paths been instructed to cross?

Jones

He lowered his head,
Looking into my troubled mind.
His death was justified by my cause.

His aura dwelled within me,
My visions unified with his.
My confusion regarding him subsided,
My questions were all answered
Through the silence of his voice.

His purpose, his birth, his death;
All to cleanse the sins I unleashed.
The repenting process had begun.
With his death, his story and teachings
Would be heard by all.

God's plan, to increase faith
Through the rise and fall of sin,
Through the evil of one
And the glory of the other.

My visions became blurred;
My mind circled an endless pit.
My arms became numb as I sat down for stability.
I could only look to the Son with more envy;
He had understood his task the whole time,
Whereas I did not.

The longer I remained before him,
The more resentful I became.
My role in God's plan disgusted me.
My hand aided in my own undoing.
My scars, my torture, my pain;
All a part of the plan,
All cleansed amongst the living
Within the death of the chosen one.

The Harvester

Every drop of his blood that fell
Upon the hot sand was a cleansing of sins.
He was born from the sins of man;
He died for the sins of man.

I was only a pawn.
    I was no different than the others.
    For that, I became enraged.
    I wanted the Son to live,
    To not fulfill his destiny of death.
    My words were pointless,
    As God's plan would always progress.

The guards who stood at a distance; all pawns.
    The pleading peasants; all pawns.
    The kings and shepherds; all pawns.
    The traveling nomads; all pawns,
    The faithful disciples; all pawns,
    The worshipping congregation; all pawns.
    My seven demons; all pawns.
    My whole existence was a lie.

My confusion rose to heights unknown.
    I became drunk with a thirst for blood.
    Death was a lingering thought that I could relate to.
    I turned to the city to appease my appetite.

The disciples all met a swift death,
    What I received next would be a blessing.
    From around the corner, he collided with me.
    His tongue babbling, his pulse quickening.
    Full of remorse for what he had done to his master,
    He sweated profusely with resentment.

Upon bumping into one another,
    His bag of coins spilled to the ground.
    His fingers scraped the dirt to retrieve his payment.

Jones

He was in a panic.
My hand around his throat increased his dread.

Dragging him through the corridors,
    He pleaded with me that he had nothing to do
    With the death of the son,
    But I knew otherwise.

As his neck stretched against the rope,
    I did not see his soul.
    As he swung lifeless in the air,
    His soul did not come to me.
    With my blade, I sliced open his chest.
    He had already repented for his sins.
    I was denied my corrupted disciple.

There was nothing more I needed from the city.
    The mourning and worshipping of the Son
    Only angered me more.
    His tale and purpose was what I came for,
    And the answer was what I left with.

I found sanctuary back within my realm.
    I was lost.

My once great demented religion began to suffer.
    The land and all of its inhabitants became his.
    Acts of man were done so in his name.
    Temptation became a rarity.
    The sacrifice for mankind was a strong tale of honor,
    Of which lessened my importance.

Society looked upon the sinners with eyes of judgment
    And swift discipline based on laws.
    Slowly, I was being washed from the walls of civilization
    Through the religious practices

The Harvester

And the understanding
That I was the opposite path against the glory.

A sudden shift from my realm
　Led the dead far from my clutches.
　With an approaching death,
　The preachers would visit the weak
　And allow them to repent against their sins
　Thus gaining them entry through the gates of Heaven.

I became mindless with my intentions.
　I became pointless with my words.
　My sins were useless to mankind.
　I was useless.

I plummeted deep into a trench of depression.
　The lack of guidance;
　The lack of understanding;
　The lack of hearing my prayers
　Led to my fall from grace.

The mere thought of repenting against one's sins
　Deeply destroyed my inner most thoughts.
　I could not overlook the cause;
　I could not overlook the Son
　And the fact that all I had achieved
　Was for the sake of him.

My anger became irrational,
　My temper without a ceiling.
　I was left alone to understand the path.

I was not meant to comprehend the role
　In which I played.
　I was not meant to reflect upon
　All that I had done.

Jones

I was meant to merely progress along my path
Without crossroads, without concern.

Who was I to question God?
    Who was I to challenge the plan?
    Within my realm I resided,
    Awaiting the arrival of my own fate,
    As my welcome upon the land was surely ending.

God had left me.
    He left to tend to his Son.
    Once, I was his task;
    I was the cherished one who needed guidance.
    I was the Lamb, the prosperous one;
    Tasked with the inevitable,
    Trusted with man against my palm.

I wanted to slumber within the darkness of Hell,
    Awakened only when my death should arrive.
    Stirred only when I should be judged for my life.
    Until then, I offered no good will toward man.

I had become numb to the civility of mankind.
    I had seen a soul destroy another
    With violence only man could do.
    I had seen the same soul repent upon death's edge.
    Free from punishment, free from pain,
    Granted access through the gates of the holy kingdom.
    The ability to deny sinful actions that the mind
    Would never forget or forgive the body for.
    Sinners should be denied entry,
    Sent to me for judgment.
    My path should not be ignored
    Based on false words of the tongue,
    Through the frightened, babbling mouths
    Of those near death.

The Harvester

There should be no remorse for sinners.
    Their choices robbed them of that opportunity.
    The way their ears perked upon hearing my whispers,
    Stole their good and twisted it beyond repair.
    A path never turns around;
    It only progresses further away.
    If the sinners were remorseful,
    They would have not heard my call in the first place.
    They would have not listened to my name.
    They would have had eyes focused on God.
    They would have had ears only for the strong.
    Instead, they welcomed me into their hearts.
    They guided me through their visions.

They chose my tale over his.
    They believed my words against his.
    They entrusted me and not him.
    They followed me and watched as he walked away.
    They were mine for the reaping, not for his salvation.

Within the religion of man,
    My name became that of an embattled demon
    Denied access to the glory land.
    Once an angel of God,
    Damned from his kingdom for tempting man with sin.
    I became a hoofed man with a horned temple,
    So disgusting that only the shadows
    Would cast eyes upon me.

I became a symbol of evil,
    A fallen spirit exiled by the hand of God.
    My tale was unjust and wrongfully told.
    I was no serpent within the garden.
    I was no angel forsaken by God.
    I was a servant to him, summoned to unleash sin.
    I was damned through my own misconception.

Jones

My hatred for man only grew
    With every sermon that falsely told my tale.
    My true story hidden beneath the glory of the Son;
    Denied by ears of the worshippers.
    My words meant nothing in return.

I ponder the reaction of society if they knew my destiny.
    That their God purposely bred sin to tempt their faith.
    Only to allow to repent through the death of his Son.
    Would they follow him? Would they worship him?
    The death, the dismay, the chaos that occurred
    While sin was unleashed.

It was of no wonder why the true words
    Were unknown from the teachings of religion.
    The amount of sinners unable to repent as their deaths
    Had been prior to the religious awakening,
    The sufferers were denied the gates of glory.
    No retribution, no reclamation.
    Their souls would be as scorned as I.
    True disciples discarded
    Surviving on vengeance and retaliation.

I will not bow down and deny my own existence.
    I will not allow my tale to go untold.
    I will not shelter my emotions
    As I am portrayed as a crimson goat.

The tale of the Lamb did not end with his captured death.
    The plan was for him to die for the sins of mankind
    And to allow each person to renew faith.
    He was to rise again for the salvation of man.

A bright religion spread across the land.
    The new religion spoke of a righteous path,

The Harvester

One free from the temptations of sin.
God became more difficult to behold
As the release of sin forced many to stray,
But the act of repenting allowed for their return.

Churches were constructed
  In every village and city to show faith.
  The worthy grew during the enlightening era.
  Sinners were frowned upon
  As if they had a contagious plague.
  My name was shunned by most ears.
  The mere mention of it
  Was punishable through damnation.

The dead were celebrated and mourned,
  But praised as they would sit next to the Lord.
  Their bodies buried in nature's ground.
  The process irritated me.

After the glorious religion was upheld,
  My realm no longer received the roaming dead.
  Although I did despise the wandering dead,
  My realm would not function the same without them.
  My filtration fields had nothing to filter.
  My river had nothing to feast upon.
  Hell began to starve.

To allow the survival of my kingdom,
  I added idealism to the process of the new dead.
  Upon burial, my Reapers visited every grave,
  Every tomb, and every coffin
  And stripped the corpse of their flesh,
  Leaving behind only bones.

Jones

The skeletal remains became a symbol of death for religion
    And translated as the flesh and soul were one.
    Unfortunately that was untrue.
    Their soul may have gone to Heaven,
    But their flesh was to be devoured by my river.
    I was forced to steal the dead back for my own.
    All of my once provided resources were gone.
    My kingdom was suffering,
    Being choked from existence.
    The only travelers within my realm
    Were those who fell victim to sin
    And refused to repent before God.

Within the once great city of Hell, I resided.
    Seeking salvation I entered my underground sanctuary.
    The moistened, dark atmosphere pleased me
    And took me back to my origin within the city.

Cowering within my own self-pity
    Was not where I desired to find myself again.
    I recalled the anger of God when I stole his city.
    The mountains cracked and the seas split.
    A complete disfiguration of the land.
    His trees were uprooted; his animals were killed.
    All of his creations bled that day.

To conjure that much anger through such little effort
    Made me ponder how much God could be angered
    And how much pain would be inflicted.

The city was isolated between the seas and mountains.
    Nature was the only victim.
    Could God be angered enough to expand his tremors;
    To deepen his trenches?

The Harvester

I could not simply steal another city;
    I required the humans for my task.
    A downfall of mankind in the eyes of God.
    A fall from grace, an overshadowing of faith;
    A denial of the Son.
    To have his own Son die for the sins of mankind
    And have the humans continuing sinning?
    The idealism would disgust God
    Who would have no choice, but to show his anger
    Through violent storms and shattering earthquakes.
    I would have battles in the name of religion;
    Death in the name of the Son.

The earth would deteriorate
    Underneath the hands of the mortals,
    So much so that God would have to intervene.
    Lands would be left scarce and wasted.
    The hand of man would scar the planet.
    Populations would be bred through sin
    Like an encroaching infestation.

Anger was what I demanded from God.
    The same anger I had felt through his servants.
    The same anger I had felt through my sins.
    The same anger I had felt
    Through my understanding of his Son.

The worshippers of the Son
    Were busily transcribing the tale of the new religion.
    Hidden well from the eyes of civilization, they wrote.
    Hidden well from the stars in the sky, they wrote.

Much like at the manger,
    I was not welcomed upon the same terrain.
    They were well guarded with God's servants,
    But that did not alter my desire to see for myself.

Jones

A book, a tale, a story for the prosperity of religion.
The words were to be holy
And uninfected by any whispers of sin.
Scrolls were being written upon
Within various locations on the land.
They had gone to great lengths to conceal its origin,
But that did not reduce my curiosity.

Within the eastern lands, I came upon a cave
Marked only by torches and secured with two guards.
My feet shifted through the sands,
My cloak trailing through an increasing wind.
My scythe glistening from the moon.
The darkness hid me well
Until I entered the circle of torches.

The guards gripped their swords,
Holding them steady towards me.
A brief look into their eyes
Told me that they were servants of God
Burdened to protect the book
And those who transcribed the pages.

The moon fled from the sky
Taking the sparkling stars along with it.
Clouds rolled through the night like galloping horses.
The sands sifted through the air,
Trying to persuade me to turn away.
The dense, grainy wind tore at my exposed skin.
The cloth in my cloak frayed and split,
But my feet remained still.

My intentions were to make it known that
Nothing shall be hidden from me;
Nothing shall be forbidden from my eyes.
I had been left confused for much too long.
I could hear the words of those with the scroll.

The Harvester

The wind gifted me with their mind's thoughts.
They spoke of the origins of earth;
They spoke of God's creations.

With my ear to the wind,
The sands became more violent;
The guards stepped toward me.
God knew I was listening and ordered my removal.
Their swords and armored boots pushed me back
To where my ears no longer heard the thoughts.

I dreamed of plaguing the minds
Of those who transcribed the words.
To corrupt the very foundation of the new religion
Through the twisted words of the worshippers.
Alas, God had foreseen my own temptations
And prepared well for the possibility.

I traveled to all the areas where the scrolls
Were being transcribed and received the same greeting.
A feeling of unwelcoming,
Of disapproval through the winds.

If God objected of my venturing,
Of my existence after my task was completed,
He would greatly disapprove of what was to come.
My offering of a life in black would be granted to all.

My next actions would upset
The establishment of the new religion
And forever change the thought patterns of man.
The book would be my enemy,
But also serve as my research.
The book would guide me to the weaknesses
And allow me entry into the worshipper's mindset.

Jones

I would serve as the demon they portrayed me to be.
    I would serve as the evilness that prowled the land.
    Chaos would be gifted to the otherwise content
    By acknowledgment of my being.
    They would alter my tale to appease their book,
    They concealed the side of God deemed unspiritual,
    But I would spread the true word.

I cannot undo what was already transcribed,
    But my vengeance would serve as my infliction.
    The concealment of the truth would be my uprising.
    The practice of their faith
    Would be lost along with their prayers.
    No doubt, the book would serve them well
    As it was relatable to their simple mortal minds.
    It would bring about an understanding of death
    And the glory they would receive within Heaven,
    But there would be a darker side too,
    One that is not understood.
    One that the mind could not envision.
    There would be a side that would not be transcribed;
    That would not be practiced in the congregations.
    A side full of shadows, far from the eyes,
    Far from the depicted angels.
    One where flesh would serve as a meal;
    Where bones would be discarded.

Most will never know the darkened side of the religion,
    The one they worship and follow without guidance.
    Their prayers would be that of kindness and affluence.
    Full of warm sun and cool wind.
    They sought to kneel beside him on his throne,
    To stand before him in righteousness.
    They long for their eyes to behold him,
    For their throats to drink his wine.

The Harvester

Would they be as faithful if the book spoke of the truth?
 Would they still worship
 If the book told the full tale?
 Would they walk the path
 If the book revealed the alternative?
 We shall see.

VI. Defiance

I was at another crossroad.
As sinners walked through the glory of Heaven,
I walked amongst my fields.
As the damned envisioned God's valleys,
I walked amongst my fields.
As the unjust stood before the gates of God,
I stood alone before mine.

I knelt upon the path and prayed,
To whom I did not know.
I prayed for the truth, for the understanding,
But mostly I prayed for the strength.

I had no successes; only failures.
I was immortal, but dead inside.
The sins, the demons, the choices;
All for nothing.

The release of sin upon man was foreseen.
The acceptance of sin by man was foreseen.
The birth and death of the Lamb was foreseen.
My demise was foreseen.

The Harvester

I had no more depression.
    Resentment was what flowed through me.
    A disgust for Heaven
    And all who walked amongst her fields.

I had no sorrow for myself.
    I had no hatred for the Son;
    He too was a part of the plan.
    As I kneeled in Hell,
    I knew my tale had not yet ended.
    Surrounded by death, the humans became my enemy.
    They had not experienced the glory of my existence.
    They had not experienced the hatred of my hand.
    Sheltered sins of a scripted plan would not suffice.
    Acceptance from God no longer plagued my mind.
    If, indeed, the humans desired sin
    Then they would be granted just that.

The seven sins would be amended.
    The sins of God were accepted by all.
    My sins would provide another path.
    A path of separation from the kingdom.

I would twist the original sins into my own
    To where the edge of good and evil
    Would be a thin crevice.

I opened my eyes to reveal each of my fellow demons.
    I did not need to speak;
    They knew of my intentions.
    I offered them each a choice.
    To repent for their sins and return to God
    Or journey with me one last time.
    I would not be ashamed of their answers.
    My respect for each of them was too strong
    To alter my feelings toward them.

Jones

I could not demand their fall.
  I could not demand their denial of God.
  Each would be gifted passage from my realm
  Followed by my admiration and acceptance.

They were each servants of God before my rise.
  The plan of God was successful,
  But fate had extended my purpose—not theirs.

As each kneeled before me, their decisions became clear;
  Our destinies became one.
  We would not fall victim to repenting.
  We would not deny who we were.

We all went our separate ways,
  With the task to spread more sin upon mankind.
  Pure sin was our weapon.
  Sin that would alter the foundation of society.
  A blanket of evilness that would cover the land.

No more individual sin toward individual man.
  Mass wrath, mass greed, mass sloth,
  Mass gluttony, mass lust, mass envy
  And mass pride would fall upon the world.
  We would reveal ourselves to back the tales.
  We would make it so that God's gifts were unattainable,
  And all would be infected.
  Throughout the land, my fellow demons went.
  With minds full of sin,
  They headed out—all but Lucifer,
  Who remained within Hell.

After they had departed,
  I traveled to the banks of the troubled river.
  It could sense my sorrow; it could feel my pain.
  The tides were the calmest I had ever seen.

The Harvester

The ferry slowly sailed towards the dock
As I awaited the arrival of the blacksmith.
No words were spoken
As the vessel carried me to the other side.

With foot upon the banks, the ferryman
    Allowed the river's hunger to crumble the docks.
    With staff in hand, he bowed before me.
    I was not in need of his services anymore.
    His soul was mine, but his heart belonged to another.
    If given a choice, he would've stayed by my side,
    But I did not offer him one.
    By releasing the grip on his soul,
    I allowed him to exit Hell,
    And begin a quest in search of his beloved.
    With no master, the river buckled the hardened ferry
    Allowing current to overcome the vessel.

Gripping my scythe tightly, I climbed the rocky cliffs
    And came to the fields of bone outlining the city.
    No wandering souls, no howls of the dead;
    Only peace.

The city; the relic of my endeavors stood bare
    The cells of my prison emptied.
    The corridors of the courtyard were vacant.
    Lucifer appeared alongside me as my pride was strong.
    I often pondered my choice, whether it was wise or not,
    But Lucifer reminded me of pride through memories.
    An acknowledgment of acceptance,
    An acknowledgment of gratitude for all I had done.
    Never before had someone granted me understanding.
    I accomplished everything God intended me to do.
    If not for me, the Lamb would not exist.
    If not for me, mankind would not have sinned.
    If not for me, society's faith would not be tested.

Jones

God owed me;
The Lamb owed me all that I had lost.

My reclamation would be in the form of sin upon man.
　　The population responsible for the death of God's Son.
　　I would prove to both
　　That man was not capable of repenting.
　　Death of sinners should be mine for the control.
　　Those who follow me
　　Should not be given another chance.
　　They will be damned to me for all eternity.
　　My kingdom shall prosper once again.

Lucifer and I overlooked the skulls of the goats.
　　The horns of the animal protruding from the dirt,
　　Their hallowed eyes staring back at us.
　　We stood at the threshold of a great challenge,
　　One that would destroy all of us.
　　A purpose more meaningful than I alone.
　　An idealism that would forever separate my kingdom
　　And split the reality of the human civilization.
　　As the congregations distorted my image
　　And destroyed my tale, my name still lingered.
　　My shadow still lurked in the darkness.
　　A threat of awareness, but society would have no idea
　　Or warning as to what bombardment lay ahead,
　　An Age of Evil.

It was time for me to leave
　　And realize my full potential.
　　Lucifer stayed behind in the city
　　And awaited any outcome that approached.
　　An honor much obliged from the once great angel.

The Harvester

I ventured to a valley between two mountain ranges.
    The tall trees were full of life,
    Swaying beneath the warmth of the sun.
    Their leaves were that of the brightest green.
    Their bark was a wonderment for any palm to touch.
    Hidden well from the greedy human hands,
    Nature was untainted and serene.
    A true essence for what the world was meant to be.
    The roof of the trees hid my travels from the sky.
    The sun's rays could only capture hints of movement.
    With every stream of light that pierced the trees,
    They tried desperately to understand my intentions.
    The winds shifted the trees in order to view me,
    But the thickened vegetation was too difficult to bend.
    The shadows were my guide.
    Knowing what they shielded from their creator,
    Caused the trees much suffering and despair.
    Their twisting trunks moaned as I passed;
    Their branches trembled as I walked.

All animals fled as I passed.
    Much like an approaching storm,
    The animals foresaw my intentions, too,
    And made haste far from the valley.
    Still the sun tried desperately to see me,
    But my path snaked between the trees at random.
    With a sharpened scythe across my back and
    A rusty chain in hand, I was not ready to be seen.

The chain was attached to a well-known prophet
    Who I pulled behind me.
    The tightened links choked his throat.
    His hands clamoring for freedom;
    His feet struggled to stay afoot.
    The trees wept with their fallen leaves.
    Their roots unearthed in hopes to hinder my travels.

Jones

The prophet pleaded with me for his release.
    He offered me the opportunity to repent.
    I grinned at his offer.
    He promised me prayer in solitude.
    I tightened the chain in hopes
    Of halting his babbling tongue.

We reached the edge of the forest;
    The edge of my sheltering.
    With my next footstep, I would begin my fate.
    The skies would no longer be confused as to my actions.
    I could see the edge of the sunlight upon the ground,
    A crossroad per say.
    The height of the trees and the angle of the sun
    Created a perfect line serving as my judgment.

My demons awaited my next step.
    One step would begin the fall of mankind.
    One foot would battle the righteousness of the Lamb.

I took a deep breath and smelt Heaven.
    A last temptation,
    A fleeting hope to protect the plan, I'm sure.
    I could taste the sweet nectar of the orchards.
    My tongue moistened with the aroma of wine.
    A cool breeze nestled within my beard,
    Soothing my hardened, scarred skin.

My farmland appeared in the distance.
    Fields of wheat, populated with livestock.
    The vision hesitated me,
    But I knew the memory was not mine.
    Much like everything else gifted to my mind,
    They were visions to keep me humbled,
    To prevent me from straying from the path.

The Harvester

With a lone step that would be heard across the land,
    My foot broke into the sunlight.
    I stared at the skies as I entered the circle of light,
    Pulling the rusty chain of my prisoner.

With myself and the prophet out of the forest,
    They sky quickly grew dim.
    The wind increased to stumble my approach.
    Within the middle of the circle,
    I held the prophet before me
    And pushed his face to the dirt with my foot.
    He would prove my disobedience.
    He would serve as my means to an end.

As the clouds thickened to black, I waited.
    As the mountains trembled in anger, I waited.
    As the ground shook in rebellion, I waited.

I needed to hear her song before I did anything else.
    I needed to know she was approaching.
    With nothing but the wind chiming,
    I brandished my weapon, lifted the prophet's head
    And rested his throat upon the sharpened metal.

The sky roared, and the earth began to crack.
    Tears flowed down the prophet's face.
    Filtering out the thunder and lightning,
    I was focused upon the wind,
    The only vessel that would aid her song.
    If I was indeed always within her reach,
    Then it would not be long before she arrived.
    My cloak flapped in the blistering wind.
    My foot sank deeper into the back of the prophet,
    Applying more pressure to his neck.

Jones

From a distance, I heard it.
　　That faint sound of her hymn from behind the trees.
　　I no longer feared her;
　　I no longer dwelled in her existence.
　　She would have my turmoil no longer.

Her hymn grew louder
　　As I saw her emerge from the trees.
　　I did not look upon her beauty with awe.
　　I greeted her with a disrespectful grin,
　　But she did not arrive alone,
　　A second hymn echoed hers.

Soon my ears detected several hymns
　　As different banshees joined the first.
　　My throat dried; my tongue clamored to swallow
　　As three servants of God stood around me.
　　Their lips hummed as they gazed to the prophet,
　　Projecting the visions back to God.

One knelt down to the face of the prophet.
　　I tightened my grip upon the scythe,
　　Prompting her to go no lower.
　　The banshees snarled with disgust.
　　They longed to tear the flesh from my bones,
　　But they remained at a distance
　　As my blade caressed the soft skin of the prophet.
　　My mannerism became relaxed;
　　I had something they wanted.

They gestured toward the ground, desiring me to kneel.
　　Perhaps an opportunity to repent for all I had done.
　　I saw it as a denial of all I had accomplished.

No, I would not kneel,
　　And I had demands of my own.

The Harvester

I demanded a safe haven for my demons.
The mouths of the banshees all rejected my words.
I demanded the return of my farmland.
The mouths of the banshees all rejected my words.
I demanded the destruction of the repenting process.
The mouths of the banshees all rejected my words.

With all my demands shunned,
    I had nothing else to live for.
    All my hopes cast aside without much thought.
    My disappointment with being nothing
    Boiled my skin and enraged my heart.
    All that I had once believed in was gone.
    All that I had once cherished was corrupted.
    The weeping prophet embodied all of it.
    All of the emotions; all of the chaos.

I had one more demand.
    With a clear voice and eager tongue,
    I looked to the sky so that God could see my face.
    I demanded that the prophet shall symbolize
    All that was truly wrong with God's plan
    And for my tale to be forever told within the shadows
    Despite how bright the sun would shine.

With an upward pull, my blade tore through his throat.
    The prophet's separated head arched upward
    Trailed by streams of blood.
    The four banshees screamed violently,
    Awaiting their next command.

The clouds cried with vengeance.
    The mountains erupted with a smoldering release.
    There was no avoiding my fall.
    My blade chose my new destiny;
    My new path away from God.

Jones

I could see the new task
    Of the banshees written upon their faces.
    My retrieval, my capture.
    Neither of which I would allow.

The banshee behind me reached for my shoulders,
    My scythe removed her ability to touch.
    Two banshees lunged for me;
    Their strength was admirable
    And I had no choice but to fly upward with them.

The force in which they pulled me was mind altering,
    But I still held my weapon.
    With a heavy swing, I raised my scythe ahead of one
    And allowed its release to fall back down.
    I continued to pull downward
    In hopes to carve my way through her back.
    Every tug sliced deeper,
    Prompting blood curdling screams.

I dropped back to the ground
    As another one landed before me.
    My personal guide; the one who tormented me.
    Her breath was bitter sweet;
    Her mannerisms were as pure of hate as could be.
    Her beauty was mind numbing, but did not distract me
    As I stood there covered in the blood of her allies.

There was no weakness within my veins;
    No fear of past encounters with her.
    There was only hatred for all that she had done.
    The cave, the village, the pain.

My disobedience was justified.
    Her hesitation only halted her failure.
    Her hesitation strengthened me
    As she pondered God's demands.

The Harvester

With her deep in thought and hearing God's plan,
    I stepped over to the beheaded prophet,
    Cleansing the blade upon his cloth.
    Her head tilted up to the sky, her eyes full of doubt.

As she lunged for me, I lowered and swung my weapon.
    The rotation severed both her legs as she sailed over me.
    I twisted the handle, set the blade upright.
    She landed on the sharpened edge.
    Her eyes drifted while watching her soul escape.

Covered in the blood of the servants,
    Surrounded by the corpse of banshees and the prophet,
    I waited.

The earth shook.
    A large crack split the sky
    As if hands were prying the clouds apart.
    Through the crevice they crept in, the Angels of God.
    They swarmed through the trench, scouring the sky.
    They landed within the valley, surrounding me on all sides.

In unison, they gestured for me to kneel.
    Again I denied their request.
    I could feel God's frustration growing.
    I could see it within the eyes of his angels.
    The valley was filled with his servants.

To test my intentions,
    God commanded one lone angel to approach.
    Her demeanor was kind and gentle,
    But her backing was not the same.
    Unlike the banshee, she was of no individual thought.
    Her face was a lie; her smile was not hers.

Jones

The sun casted a beautiful haze upon her skin.
    The wind lifted her hair in a golden glory.
    My face displayed that of acceptance.
    My eyes were full of understanding,
    But my mind was unaltered.

She was still too far from me.
    My weapon was not long enough to reach her.
    I swallowed excessively to portray weakness;
    She moved closer.
    My head bent downwards;
    She moved closer.
    I took several deep breaths;
    She moved closer.

She was still too far away, so I laid my weapon down.
    Not to concede, but to measure the distance.
    I fell to my knees as she neared.
    I needed her feet to cross my blade.
    My hand rested on the lowest portion of the handle.
    My head remained bowed down,
    But my eyes stared at the blade.
    Her footsteps trampled the grass
    As she cautiously walked towards me.

With one foot, she stepped over my blade.
    Her second foot followed closely after.
    I closed my eyes and calmed my heart.
    My palm was steady; my arm was strong.
    With a pull of the weapon,
    The blade sliced through the grass
    And relieved her feet from her legs.
    The screams from all the angels disrupted the wind.

I slammed my fist deep into the ground,
    Creating a crevice wide enough to swallow myself.

The Harvester

I fell down into the caverns of my realm,
Far from the clutches of the angels.
The land above shook with God's anger.
The screams of the angels
Followed me down into the darkness.

I traveled deep into the belly of the earth
    Until I met my solitude in a darkened cave.
    My location unknown to the sky and even to myself.
    I only desired to be hidden from their reach.

With blood of my enemy clinging to my hands,
    I reached into my satchel for my tools.
    Much like the beginning,
    I possessed only a quill, candle and parchment.
    It was fitting that my fall shall be the same as my rise.

I write not for the benefit of God or myself.
    I write to continue my story; to continue sin.
    To tell the story of my demons
    And to prove the existence of my realm.
    I write to battle and entrap those who repent.
    My sins would live on well past my time
    Through the visions and corrupt minds of the humans.

A dirt filled stream became my eyes into the world;
    Brushing aside the stones, I used the water like a mirror
    To witness the actions of my demons.
    Their fall from God would be my own.
    Their defiance would serve as my sentence.

Like a window to the soul, I could watch
    As Amon fled to the largest city to the north.
    She arrived at the gates with nothing more
    Than a pure hatred for society
    And a dagger within each hand.

Jones

Her essence captivated the crowds.
  Her stride sealed the fates of many.
  Her scent of wrath filled the lungs of all who were near.
  The once peaceful citizens turned on one another.
  The corridors were filled with violent acts of murder
  And condemned thoughts towards their fellow man.

Armored guards were no match for her skill.
  The city revolted with the sinful thoughts of corruption.
  She made no attempt to hide herself;
  She made no excuse for what she was.
  Terror was what she gifted those left alive.
  The instability of why God would allow such a deed.
  The question that would plague the land.

The sky turned black from the swarm of angels.
  The servants of God funneled into the awaiting city.
  As the people scattered for safety, Amon did not.
  She stood dripping with mortal blood for all to see;
  For all to carry on her story and existence.
  Surrounded by the angels, she took off her cloak
  To reveal two leather straps holding more daggers.
  The angels converged upon her with retribution.
  Each of her blades forced an angel to retreat,
  But as one fled, others appeared.

Amon sliced through the flesh with honor
  And the backing of her true wrath.
  She continued her infliction of pain,
  But soon slowed as the mass of angels increased.

The darkened shadows cast by their wings
  Shielded my eyes from her capture.

The Harvester

I could see Mammon.
 He had made great strides in corrupting
 The kings of two rivaling kingdoms,
 Who each greedily desired the land of the other.
 Their massive armies marched to an adjacent valley.
 Their battle flags danced within the wind;
 Their horses and soldiers stood strong,
 Each prepared to die for their king.
 The prowling nature of Mammon
 Had him riding horseback amongst one of the armies.
 The kings sat hillside safely from the battle.
 Signaling their armies into war
 Was as easy as raising their hands.

The valley shook as the large armies ran toward each other.
 Swords clashed as blood spilled.
 The two armies were well matched in size.
 Catapults tossed large boulders onto the awaiting crowd
 Burying those unfortunate to be in their paths.
 Fire tipped arrows soared through the air.

No one king would control the valley;
 No one king would feel the victory.
 As the clouds parted,
 The servants of God swarmed down the mountains.
 The slow grey death approached
 Like a violent storm creeping across the sea.

The grave vision poured into the valley.
 Swords halted, anger subsided.
 The unnatural flock of angels
 Reduced all in the valley to that of a common man.
 No armies, no sides, no enemies; only human.
 No longer threatened by their common man,
 The soldiers fled.

Jones

Fear struck the two groups as the angels flew.
    Death was quickly delivered to the mortals.
    The sky became a storm of the living
    While the land was drenched with corpses.
    Within moments, both armies were slaughtered.
    The piles of the dead littered the land.

Mammon was hidden beneath a large pile of the dead.
    He remained silent,
    But the angels could hear his beating heart.
    One by one his cover of carcasses was reduced.
    He soon was extracted by an angel grasping his ankle.
    He kicked himself free and clawed across the corpses,
    But others converged upon him.
    Held tightly, they took him into the sky.

I lived vicariously as a new image revealed itself
    Within the crust of my underground salvation.
    I watched as Belphegor infected society with sloth.
    He tempted preachers and their congregations
    With lack of prayer and remorse toward the Son.
    He constructed the ability for mankind
    To worship only when they desired something in return.
    A despicable act against those devoted to their Lord.
    Religion ventured away from a daily practice
    And was soon hidden from those once faithful.

Prayer became an aftermath,
    A consuming action easily cast aside.
    Corruption amongst the preachers
    Rose to an unstable foundation.
    Doubt lingered among the congregations.
    The hatred toward those not of the same faith
    Arose once again with Belphegor disrupting the waters.

The Harvester

Belphegor split his time between many preachers
    Until the skies blackened.
    Each of the preachers blamed the other
    As the sky tore apart and the angels descended.
    Confident that God would punish those who differ,
    Each preacher believed they summoned the angels.

Every corridor was searched,
    Every door ripped from the hinges.
    Sensing his end was near, Belphegor arose from hiding
    Wearing the white robe of a preacher.
    With no resistance, his deed was done.
    The angels clung to Belphegor as they lifted him.
    He left the city with judging eyes and deceptive ears.
    He granted society with religious options,
    All which would slow their paths.

The cave gifted me the view of Beelzebub.
    I watched as he took to the farmlands with gluttony.
    He whispered to all who would hear
    His plans for poaching and waste.
    To live in excess far from what one needed to survive.
    Each city he visited became overridden
    With contaminated food and poisoned waterways.
    Civil disgust became apparent as edible food
    Became scarce and a luxury for only the wealthy.
    The poor became hungry while the rich fed like pigs.

The hides of rare species became desirable.
    All of God's creatures were salvageable,
    From his beloved antelopes to the beasts of the plains.
    Hunters spread upon the land to earn coin.
    Species slowly became extinct.
    God's retribution was in the form of disastrous storms

That uprooted vegetation and altered the terrain.
Floods chased his creations away from the hunters
Into distant lands where more poachers awaited.

Angered by the disobedient humans,
God allowed his waters to flood the cities.
The bloated corpses were drained from the streets
As the waters lowered back into the seas.

After the storms subsided, mankind still hunted.
The expanding kingdoms toppled trees without care.
Piles of decayed wood were left to suffocate God's land.

The waste hid the streets of the cities.
There was no more admiration of God's land,
Only a resource to be drained to benefit civilization.

With the angels approaching across the seas
Shadowing the natural blue hue of the water,
Beelzebub ran from the city and hid in a hallowed tree.
The angels followed his scent, grabbed him by the neck,
And escorted him to the clouds.

My heart bled with remembrance of my own lust
As I peered deeper into the blood stained stream.
As fast as her aged legs could carry her,
Asmodeus entered into a village toting her sin.

With vials of potions,
Asmodeus contaminated the water source.
The following night as the villagers drank,
Sin spread through their veins
With emotions sprinting through their mortal minds.
The passions of the mind were allowed freedom.
A release from the binds that tie the heart.

The Harvester

Asmodeus stayed near
   As the villagers despised their mates
   And fell victim to their temptations.
   They each desired someone they could not have.
   The sanctuary of relationships was punished
   And betrayed by those who chose the different path.
   Their desires were no longer unattainable
   As their actions were fulfilling their minds.

Asmodeus could only watch
   As the wings of the angels glistened in the moonlight.
   She could not outrun them.

With cane in hand,
   Asmodeus stood before the angels in silence.
   As one reached for her,
   She struck it across the face with her cane.
   Her frail body was pulled up to the sky.

◦❦◦

My blurred vision portrayed a familiar image from my past.
   Leviathan never overstayed his welcome in a village.
   He whispered his envious visions to those in his way.
   Left behind was the beginning of thievery and jealously.
   Nightly thefts became a ritual.

Hidden shadows shielded the condemned
   As the night gave way to abundant crimes.
   Doors became blockaded to protect possessions.
   City guards were of no assistance,
   As the fingers of corruption had a far reach.
   The poor stole from the rich;
   The rich stole from the rich.
   With so much corruption,
   Cities became plagued with violence

Jones

With an angel scout calling forth the others,
  Levi tempted the group leaders to the city center.
  Visions of thieving visitors were portrayed.
  Full belief was given to the whispers.

The winged sky fell upon the city
  Engulfing those who dared to defend themselves.
  Like prey to the wolves, everyone was devoured.

The angels covered the city in bloodshed that night,
  But the sweet smell of sin crept through the streets.
  Everything was searched until the angels
  Came across Levi huddled behind a stack of crates.

He was dragged through the city streets.
  Through the night air, he ascended.

I felt the caverns of my realm shift.
  The vision revealed the ceiling of my realm
  Being pried apart with angels filling the outer tunnels.

The darkness clashed with their pearly white appearance
  And proved difficult for them to navigate.
  Confusion twisted its way through their minds
  And obstructed the commands of God.
  The sheer amount of them filtering
  Through the tunnels would always push forward.
  They collided with the solid walls.
  Their wings scraped against the rocky terrain,
  But still they flew.

They advanced through the labyrinth,
  Pleading with God to lead the way.
  Some flew in circles trying to understand,

The Harvester

Others wept uncontrollably with howling screams.
Those who lingered were pushed aside
To allow for the stronger ones to continue.

My enemies piled over the river
    And were met with high, cresting waves.
    Every scream prompted the others to fly higher,
    Far from the reach of the troubled current.

Into Hell they went, landing upon my walls.
    Their disgusting feet perched upon my gates.
    They glided through my city,
    Encircling the buildings like vultures.
    They searched every cell within the cavern,
    But found nothing.
    They searched every structure within the city,
    But found nothing.

Lucifer waited within the palace,
    Kneeling in the entrance room.
    Upon the floor were two double bladed scythes,
    Sharpened as only he could achieve.

He removed his cloak, revealing a bare chest.
    The wings gifted from God for his past endeavors
    Stretched to either side in a white glory.
    His long yellow hair blending with his beard.
    The angels pounded and shook the doors.

Lucifer extracted two golden daggers
    And allowed the doors to open.
    Many angels poured in before the doors shut again,
    Entrapping those inside.
    Their bodies were abused by his blades and gutted.
    The frightened souls clamored for release,
    But were clenched and swallowed by the demon.

Jones

Lucifer welcomed all who arrived
By butchering their bodies and claiming their wings.
Those who entered through the doors were devastated
With a death so troubling, even their souls were terrified.
God heard their pleas and split the land.
A vast trench tore through the ceiling of the cavern
As the sun battled with the darkness.
The river boiled with annoyance.
A ceiling trench grew directly above the palace
Where the hands of God entered
And grasped the crumbled walls.
The roof of the palace was ripped from the foundation.

Lucifer stood drenched in blood.
His wings, crimson from the onslaught.
At his feet, piles of angel corpses.
His hair dripping with blood,
He used the edge of his blade
To carve seven slices within his forearm.

His wings stretched as he grabbed his weapons.
Instead of waiting for his enemies, he took flight.
An angel corpse fell with every swing of his blades.

Holy blood rained down upon the city.
The cavern walls were painted a red hue.
The prison cells drenched in crimson.
The lifeless angels fell into the awaiting river.
Their confused souls rose through the crevice.
The continuing mass of angels
Were able to grab a hold of Lucifer,
Dampen his wing movement.
Falling to the field, Lucifer quickly arose to his feet.
The blades easily sliced through the angels.
Legs were severed, but still the angels took flight.

The Harvester

The cavern walls shook under the frustration of God.
    Lucifer took to the cavern heights again.
    Flying close to the high crevice,
    An unknown force grabbed Lucifer
    And suspended him in the air without movement.
    The attack of the angels halted as they encircled him.
    The two weapons, beyond his control,
    Fell from his clutches.

Within moments, Lucifer unleashed an angered scream
    As his wings were torn from his body.
    The feathered limbs fell alongside their owner.
    The angels watched as the demon fell into the river.

Not being permitted to sink,
    The current brought Lucifer to the surface.
    A wave washed him toward the shoreline.
    Without weapons and an unimaginable wound,
    He stood as the angels descended.

Lucifer, weakened and upon one knee,
    Could offer no more defiance to the intruders.
    Every portion of his body was held
    As he drifted to the skies.

VII. Redemption

This cave has served me well.
It has hidden me from the eyes of Heaven
Long enough to allow for my tale to be written.

My realm has been reduced to ruins.
My palace crumbled by the hand of God.
My fields destroyed with the shifting earth.
My city, savaged with no stone or skull left unturned.
My corridors, my tunnels, my caverns all devastated.
My demons, enslaved and taken to the skies.

All that crossed my threshold
Will not make the journey home.
They have willingly flown down into their graves.
I will have no mercy upon them when I steal their wings
And swallow each of their souls.
They long to obey God and serve him well,
But their eyes will never gaze upon him again.
As my goats once walked toward an unknown slaughter
So have the angels sent by their shepherd.

Those that captured my demons will be hunted.
They will not find safe haven within the clouds.
They will not find sanctuary
Within the kingdom of Heaven.

The Harvester

I will walk upon the land with the scars of my past.
    God will not be able to help those in my way.
    God will not hear the screams of those I come upon.
    God will not look over them as I stand near.

My presence will be well known within every shadow.
    Every human will hear my whispers;
    Every human will heed to my temptations.

My demons had served me well.
    Sin was altered and blindly accepted by civilization.
    I will seek their salvation in due time.

I have no more tolerance for the mortals;
    I have even less for those who repent.
    After I cleanse my realm of every winged intruder,
    I will venture upon the land,
    Finding those seeking to repent.
    I will walk upon every path toward God
    And befriend those seeking salvation.
    Those true to the path shall be ignored;
    Those who have sinned will be questioned.
    If repent spills from their mouths,
    I will reap them where they stride.
    God will not be able to help them.
    I will have no mercy upon their souls
    And will use their spines to shackle the corpses.

Much like the Lamb,
    I too will sacrifice myself for the sins of mankind.
    I too will meet my demise;
    To allow for my religion to continue upon the land.
    And I too will rise again, to acquire what is mine;
    The sinners, the damned souls, the realm, the city.

Jones

How long will God allow me to reap the humans?
How long before his anger will shatter the planet?
How long before his hand pries apart the sky?
How much damage will he tolerate?
How much blood will be allowed to spill?
I was bred to test the limitations of sin.
Now, I will test the boundaries of God.

The preachers will not speak of me as a man.
They will not speak of me as a farmer.
Instead, I will be the demon who despised God.
I will be the demon who plagued God's land.
I will be the demon who cursed God's name.
I will be the demon who fell from God's grace.

I will serve as the scapegoat for God's evils.
I will serve as the darkness to God's light.
I will serve as the death upon humanity.

I will extend my hand when God offers no guidance.
When your prayers go unanswered,
I will lend you my ear and comfort your mind.
When your dreams are troubled,
I will be there to calm your beating heart.

God will destroy in order to maintain order and peace.
The humans will thrive to seek his glory,
But with every thought lingers an option,
A choice between good and evil.

Every mortal mind will have the crossroads;
Every mortal mind will have difficult decisions.
The wind will carry my whispers;
The shadows will conceal my identity,
But I will be there upon the paths while you tread.

The Harvester

When your prayers go unanswered,
    You will summon me.
    When your dreams became shattered,
    You will summon me.
    When your life becomes unbearable,
    You will summon me.

I will come to you in your time of need.
    I will listen to you when your eyes are clouded.
    I will be there when you cannot make a decision.
    Your doubts will be my intention.
    Your emotions will be my measure.
    Your actions will be my success.

God had taught me sin and the weakness of man.
    He gave me the resource of temptation
    And the understanding of how the mind functions.
    He gave me the holes within their hearts
    And the confusion within their minds.
    He gave me the power of sin.
    He allowed my realm and the city of the dead.
    He allowed it all,
    Only if it did not interfere with his master plan.

I believed in him when I should have questioned.
    I entrusted in him when I should have doubted.
    I gave myself for his vision, for his plan.
    I gave my life for his path, for his demands.
    I gave everything for his task.

I was born much like the Son
    With a predetermined plan for life and death.
    To fulfill the demands of the task.
    A symbol to be used by humanity based upon choice.
    The choice, to sin or not.
    God knew mankind would sin.

Jones

He knew the downfall of the civilized world
Would be destroyed without a symbol of good.
If left alone within my hands,
The mortals would all enter through my realm.
The Lamb needed to rise and fall
To give a new hope and life to the land
Otherwise, the beloved humans would perish.

My mind began to question.
    My thoughts were troubling,
    My understanding of all that I had sought after
    Encircled my visions and haunted my eyes.

I saw my farmland upon the dirt floor,
    My cottage, my crops, my livestock all before me.
    The sway of the elongated stalks,
    The birds soaring within the sky.
    The branches of the trees bending within the wind.
    Loose leaves floated gracefully.

Beyond the mountains and seas of the horizons
    Were lands so beautiful to behold
    With oceans of golden wheat and abundant orchards.
    So close, but yet unattainable from my cottage.

My anger subsided and concealed itself
    As my heart bled for more visions.
    My mouth moistened with my watering eyes.
    I saw the destruction of my farm;
    I witnessed its demise.
    Why were the visions teasing my soul?

My mind cautioned me to not dwell,
    But my emotions were denying the warning.
    God knew my weakness;
    He knew the hole in my heart.

The Harvester

It served as my only temptation, my only hesitation.
The same weakness I searched for within every man.

My memories were tangled with emotions.
    All that constructed me as a man had reinvented itself.
    The feelings and the way my skin felt against the sun,
    All remnants of my farm.
    My longing to rejoin my past before I was chosen,
    Before I became who I am, before the sin,
    Before the sorrow.

I had been granted the visions for a reason I am unsure of.
    Were they to subdue my anger, to tempt me to repent?

I dwelled deeper within the visions
    Where I saw details I had never seen before.
    The horizons were blurred not from haze, but from existence.
    The mountains and oceans were distorted, but made real.
    A landscape of confusion engulfed my farm and cottage.
    A landscape isolated from any other civilization.

My eyes teased my mind with what I envisioned next.
    Small glimmers of light sparkling against the sunlight.
    Light reflecting off of concealed guards.
    Their armor returned the rays back into the sky.
    Concealed by the trees and mountains.

They were the same guards used to protect the scrolls.
    The same used behind the manger.
    The servants of God, tasked to protect the plan.
    But why my farm?

My land was not sacred; my land was not holy.
    I was nothing prior to being chosen,
    My life was peaceful and meaningless.
    My wheat fields were like all the others.

Jones

The guards never shifted, they never swayed.
They merely stood within their burden to protect.

The forests ended abruptly with a natural line
  Separating the vegetation from a vast meadow.
  The mountains were cracked in half with the same line.
  The seas edged against the same with no shoreline.
  They just ended.

My farm was not a part of human land.
  The scenery was not that of what serves man.
  The beauty was not to be shared by mortal eyes.
  My land was a part of God's kingdom,
  Far from the gates, far from where the angels soar.
  The meadows that bordered my land
  Were unlike anything seen upon the planet.
  The golden fields were that of the human dreams.
  All the faith, all the religion, all the belief.

The golden waves of the meadows,
  Home to God's own collection of livestock.
  The vision of the creatures clouded my judgment.
  My mind blocked all rational thought.
  My head would not stop spinning from doubt.
  I shielded my eyes, but the visions became stronger.
  They were unavoidable, unable to deny them.
  The goats and lambs ran through the meadows
  With a peaceful feeling of serenity and calm.
  I lost all control over my mind.

The visions cannot be true, they cannot be real.
  My farm within Heaven, the goats, the lambs.
  I tried to deny the visions by halting my writing
  And hiding within the shadows of the cave,
  But the images became brighter;
  They became inescapable.

The Harvester

I was like him.
  I was like the Son.
  He was the Lamb and I was the Goat.
  My birth was similar to his.
  The farm served as my manger.
  The goats were my kings;
  The lambs were my shepherds.
  The guards did not protect the land,
  They protected me.

I did not have the glory of his birth.
  I was born in isolation within my farm,
  Hidden from man until my task began.
  I was not to be the savior;
  I was to be the sin of the human race,
  The catalyst to begin the process.
  When God deemed me able,
  I began my life of sin within the cave.

I was the beginning of temptation,
  The beginning of hesitation.
  I served as the pawn to become the first sinner.
  All that I learned
  Would become the foundation for evil.
  All that I encountered
  Would be the knowledge
  To unleash his sins upon mankind.
  I was not the first to doubt,
  As God had doubted man's faith.
  His doubt created the plan, created my existence.

The writings of my past forged sin.
  The temptations were tested,
  The acknowledgment was understood.

Jones

I had a choice.
   A mortal life with death
   Or immortal life releasing sin.
   The crossroad that altered my being.
   The lack of understanding was the hesitation.
   God tempted me with my own sins.
   He had foreseen my choice upon my birth
   But unlike the Lamb,
   He would not allow me the understanding.
   He made me mortal within the sins.
   My decisions were of man;
   The reactions to sin would be that of man.

He gifted me nothing that I did not already have.
   Left to my own confusion,
   He sent banshees to guide me along the path.
   Pain carried me further.

He needed an evil to raise the good of the other.
   He desired a sorrow to increase the glory.
   A disturbing fear that would tempt more glorification.

He wanted a stronger faith; a stronger belief.
   Both of which were lessening amongst civilization.
   The truth hidden deep within the tale,
   Beyond the understanding of the mind.

A tale not told within the bright religion,
   Not told within the book of sermons,
   But masked within the distorted visions.

There was a relief to the understanding,
   A sense of tranquility that was cast upon me.
   An enlightenment that was welcomed,
   But I am not the chosen one, I am not the savior.
   I am the death, the reaper of souls within the plan.

The Harvester

I am the unwanted Goat used for a purpose
Then buried within the glory of the Lamb.
They both betrayed me; they both lied.
I cannot forget my past, my heritage,
My journey through sin.

My plan was foreseen
    That I would secretly fade into the shadows
    Once the Lamb was born
    As my task was deemed complete.
    They believed my disobedience would be buried.

They thought hiding the truth
    Would serve me better than knowing.
    They underestimated my pride.
    My pride within my sins;
    The pride within my demons
    Of which they will never understand.

That pride was what killed the prophet.
    That pride was what killed the banshees.
    That pride will continue my legacy.

Frustration burned deep within my heart
    As I was forced to watch the plan unfold,
    Forced into a life of sin, bred for pain
    And suffering for the purpose of human salvation.
    My eyes bled with anger.
    My ears burned with resentment.
    My misery, all for the sake of the human civilization.
    The Son would receive the glory
    And rule the kingdom of Heaven.
    I would serve as the failure,
    A mere evilness one should avoid.
    His path was foreseen,
    Mine was not worth the look.

Jones

No banshee, no sin, no pain could remove the blackness.
    To be an outsider, forsaken of the truth.
    All I wanted was the return of my farmland,
    The one that raised me;
    The one that comforted me.

My head aches with passion;
    My hands tremble with anticipation.
    As hurt as I have become, I have never felt so alive.
    Nothing hidden, nothing denied.
    What lingers behind is my anger.
    The wrath, the sin that began it all.
    Fitting that it shall be my end.

The angels are near;
    I can hear them carving through the caves.
    No more tears will be shed.
    My eyes are blistered and stained with hatred.
    My mind is bent from all I have endured.
    My body is scarred from the torture.
    All for man.

If it was a real vision all along,
    Then I will return to my farmland.
    I will travel to Heaven to retrieve what is mine.
    I will release my demons.
    If I do not receive safe passage
    Then I will forge a new path
    Under the guidance of my blade.
    I will kill as many angels as God sends.
    I will not bow down and cower within the shadows.
    I will walk amongst the humans
    And infect them all.

The Harvester

If it is faith that created the plan,
    Then I will corrupt it.
    If it is belief that God seeks from man,
    Then I will destroy it.

And if I should fail,
    My death will only serve a higher purpose.
    Much like the Lamb, I will prosper greatly
    From a mortal death within the eyes of society.
    Much like the Lamb, I will rise again.
    I will collect the souls I had lost.
    I will rebuild my kingdom.

May God help any angel within my realm.
    May the Lord help any man I come across.
    I will offer no mercy, I will offer no remorse.

I pray, not to God, not to the Son,
    But to the blade of my scythe.
    I pray that it is swift with death.
    I pray that it is steady and concise.
    I pray that upon my demise
    That I am granted the strength to live on
    Through the sins, through the deaths,
    Through the struggles of mankind.
    I pray that I alone
    Will judge the weakened souls who sin.
    I pray for the strength to never falter in my emotions,
    To never doubt.

The angels have carved a tunnel to adjoin with mine.
    Their fingers pry into the cave,
    Pulling at the rocks to gain access.
    They are tired of the darkness; they are tired of the dirt.

Jones

They long to be back within the blue skies.
Their eyes are disgusted with me.
Their anger is noticeable within every
Rock that they forcefully pull from the wall.
They want nothing more
Than to rip the flesh from my bones,
But that is not their task.
My capture is their order;
My delivery is their duty.
True servants of God,
They will not stop until they succeed.
Regardless of how many I cleanse within my realm,
There will always be more.

My beating heart will reach my land.
I will weather all storms in my way;
My death will only be within my farmland.

As the world slowly burns,
As the creation of God falls away,
As the once great human race
Slips from the graces of their Lord,
I will be there to provide understanding.

The angels stand before me now,
Hesitant in their postures.
They remain at a distance,
As God knows of my intentions.
Thousands wait within the narrow tunnel,
But only seven are present within my cave.
They have constructed a funnel for their demise.

To my quill, I pray for respect.
To my candle, I pray for acceptance.
To my scars, I pray for revenge.
To my wounds, I pray for forgiveness.

The Harvester

To my mind, I pray for understanding.
To my heart, I pray for peace.
To my blade, I pray for vengeance.

The angels remain still.
  The flame of the candle dances upon their faces
  As their eyes struggle with the darkness.

My existence is to be a lie,
  A conjured tale to appease good.
  Mankind will be easily deceived,
  But I will always know the truth.
  With a hand upon my scythe, it is time.
  It is time to alter the paths of many,
  To disturb the beautiful religion,
  To acknowledge the evil within the world,
  To justify my being and all that I have endured.

The staff of my weapon welcomes my palm.
  My fingers press against the hardened wood.
  The blade has severed many limbs,
  Has crushed many bones, has reaped many souls
  And still it emits excitement within the candlelight.
  A pride no human can understand.
  A pride God seeks from his followers.
  A pride I created and fulfilled with my destiny.
  I have what he desires; I have what his plan seeks.
  He would have to sin in order to obtain it.

A crossroad built under his ruling,
  A crossroad within Heaven itself.
  A temptation for the almighty;
  A chance for hesitation.

The choice that shaped my existence.
  The choice that binds us all together.

Jones

The choice that forges our destinies.
To sin or not to sin.

Mankind will have a choice.
    One leads to salvation, one leads to death.
    Those who remain focused
    Will stand before the Lamb.
    Those who remain confused
    Will stand before the Goat.

Regardless of the choice,
    All will be judged upon the rising.
    All will be filtered amongst the fields
    Whether they are the golden wheat of Heaven
    Or the decayed roots of Hell.

With my blade eager to rise,
    My new fate awaits.
    As the path of the angels ends,
    Mine has just begun.
    A path of death and despair.
    A path that will lead me home.

About the Author

K. Trap Jones is an author of horror novels and short stories. With inspiration from Dante Alighieri and Edgar Allan Poe, he has a temptation toward narrative folklore, classic literary works and obscure segments within society.

His novel *The Sinner* (Blood Bound Books) won the 2010 Royal Palm Literary Award. Other books include *The Drunken Exorcist* (Necro Publications), *The Crossroads* (Hazardous Press) and *One Bad Fur Day* (Sirens Call Publications).

He is also a member of the Horror Writers Association and can be found lurking around Tampa, Florida.